MW00587321
ER GIRL DOCTOR
4
BY YOSHINO ORIGUCHI
ILLUSTRATED BY Z-ton

Welcome to the Deadlich Graveyard City. We don't need doctors in this town.

DEADLICH GRAVEYARD CITY

CONTENTS

MONSTER GIRL DOCTOR

VOLUME 4

STORY BY
Yoshino Origuchi

ILLUSTRATIONS BY
Z-ton

Seven Seas Entertainment

MONSTER MUSUME NO OISHASAN VOLUME 4

First published in Japan in 2018 by SHUEISHA Inc., Tokyo.
English translation rights arranged by SHUEISHA Inc.
through TOHAN CORPORATION, Tokyo.

Seven Seas press and purchase enquiries can be sent to Marketing Manager Lianne Sentar at press@gomanga.com. Information regarding the distribution and purchase of digital editions is available from Digital Manager CK Russell at digital@gomanga.com.

Follow Seven Seas Entertainment online at sevenseasentertainment.com.

TRANSLATION: Jenn Yamazaki
ADAPTATION: Peter Adrian Behravesh
COVER DESIGN: KC Fabellon
INTERIOR LAYOUT & DESIGN: Clay Gardner
PROOFREADER: Kris Swanson, Stephanie Cohen
LIGHT NOVEL EDITOR: Nibedita Sen
MANAGING EDITOR: Julie Davis
EDITOR-IN-CHIEF: Adam Arnold
PUBLISHER: Jason DeAngelis

ISBN: 978-1-64275-056-0
Printed in Canada
First Printing: May 2019
10 9 8 7 6 5 4 3 2 1

PROLOGUE: The Amorphous Thing

THE *THING* was in trouble.

The *thing* made its constituent parts writhe, which made a gurgling sound. This was perplexing, and the sense of perplexity was the first feeling the *thing* had ever experienced.

The *thing* had nothing.

No name... Only the title given to it by the higher existence it knew as "the master."

No purpose... Directives from the master had long since ceased.

No consciousness... While the *thing* did possess thoughts, knowledge, and the ability to learn, its voluntary will was extremely sparse.

The time was midnight.

The *thing* began moving, and no one was there to stop it.

Gurgle, gurgle.

The *thing* began thinking.

The *thing* began shaking its muddy components.

At that moment, the *thing* needed to take in the nutrients required to move—it needed an external source. Once, the *thing* had been in a very comfortable place. There was no need to fear the depletion of active energy. But now, things were different. The *thing* had to move to find a new nutrient source.

Gurgle, gurgle...

The *thing* shook its body.

The *thing* divided in two from its core, in time with the subtle tremors. Without stopping, the two *things* split into four, then eight, then sixteen. No matter how many times it divided, the individual pieces were all the same size as the first—or so it seemed.

But the *thing* could feel itself growing weaker with each division. Each individual piece was probably less intelligent than when they were all collected together. But that didn't matter. If the *thing* didn't do something to break away, it would die. If everything went well, perhaps the *thing* would be able to return to a single form.

The *thing* multiplied to attain a stable life.

Each and every one of the infinite number of *thing* divisions crawled away, disappearing into the darkness of the town.

Some went to the main road.

Some went into the sewers.

Some went into the town.

As they moved, they changed. They took on forms that would allow them to go unnoticed while observing and collecting information.

The *thing* had not been given orders by anyone—it was being driven by life. How could it live most efficiently in this environment? What was the optimal method for establishing active life, rather than the parasitic one it had before?

As part of its survival strategy, the *thing* scattered into 40,000 parts, then 80,000. Each individual piece began thinking and behaving on its own.

All of this happened in the dead of the night, witnessed by no one.

CASE 01: *The Molting Lamia*

THIS IS QUITE SUDDEN, but I'd like to discuss the order of this world.

As everyone knows, there are humans, and there are monsters.

Then there are fairies.

Fairies are a species tasked with guarding the Great Fairy Queen. In other words, all other species are nothing to them. Are they humans? Or monsters? It's actually quite absurd. Among academics, the general consensus is that fairies are a type of monster, but if you ask me, this is laughably incorrect.

Fairies can only be called fairies.

They are a perfect species, a relic of the age of the gods, completely different from humans and monsters, who still have nothing but incomplete and immature civilizations. We, the fairies, are the closest things to gods in this world.

Fairies are immortal.

Fairies don't age.

Fairies fight on the front lines every single day in the battle to preserve the laws of nature.

Perhaps I should introduce myself.

I am Cottingley Bradford VI.

I have inherited the noble Bradford name, under which my predecessors served the Fairy Queen for many years, in hopes of assisting humans and monsters under her rule. The current Fairy Queen is a compassionate soul by design. Deeply concerned by the tortoise-slow speed of both human and monster civilizations' evolution, she ordered us to help them.

To comply with this order, I lead my subordinate fairies in performing our duties at a small medical facility—Litbeit Clinic. The services we brilliant fairies provide play an essential role for the humans and lamia here. The clinic's main doctor, Dr. Glenn, is as thickheaded and ignorant as you would expect a human to be. If it weren't for us, the clinic would be shut down immediately. It is only because of our secret activities that humans and monsters can go about their daily lives.

Sometimes we are called derogatory nicknames like "helper fairies," but that sort of language completely misses the point. We couldn't care less about humans and monsters. In fact, if it weren't against the Queen's will, we would be ruling over them.

"Now, everybody,"

Lady Saphentite looked down on me and my team in our perfect formation. Due to the differences in our physiques, I'm used to being looked down on. *Thou shalt not scorn the tiny races.* There is even a legend that, during the age of the gods, our lightweight stature, agility, and strength in unity allowed us to cross swords with the gods. Having a massive body means you will fall like the gigas. Our small stature is just one of the infinite facets of fairy beauty.

"Today, you won't be doing clinic work. Thank you for indulging my personal request. I have high expectations for you." Lady Saphentite expressed her gratitude to us.

It's not that I look down on all monsters. If a well-mannered lady like Sapphee has a serious request, my subordinates and I are always ready to serve.

"I appreciate your efforts," she said.

I answered Lady Saphentite on behalf of my clan.

No matter what obstacles you face, we swear on our unwavering honor as fairies that we will protect you from disaster. We understand the great honor of offering assistance, and the everlasting reward for our service...

"Yes," I said. "We will do our best."

Hmph. That's not what I was trying to say. Only simple phrases seemed to be coming out of my mouth.

We are perfect and loyal fairies, a noble species that should be ruling over the world. But we are not without weakness.

"I want to check one last time," said Lady Saphentite. "Today is a very important day for me, so I don't want Dr. Glenn to see me. Please make sure that he does not set foot in this room."

"Leave it to us!" I replied.

I had wanted to raise my hand and say, *So long as I, Cottingley Bradford VI, give the orders, the unparalleled valor of 1,000 soldiers shall serve at the lady's pleasure,* but could only manage those four words. I couldn't even enunciate those few syllables clearly, and my voice came out like a small child's.

"You're always helping me." The lady smiled and poked at my cheeks without reserve, in a way that an ordinary person could not.

I tried to resist, but my power was unable to ward off her fingers.

"Teehee! Woo!"

Even though I knew it would be useless, I wanted to scream, *Don't you know who I am? How incredibly rude of you to touch me in such a manner!* But all my words had changed to very simple phrases.

I regret to mention that there is one thing humans and monsters have that fairies do not. Fairies lack language. Of course, we can communicate with each other. But we don't have vocal cords to make the air vibrate. We possess our own unique, innate capability to exchange thoughts with each other without exchanging words. We can convey a massive amount of information and the thoughts we hold in our hearts to each other in an instant. That means we do not lie or exaggerate, and all conversations are honest and fair. It is actually a highly effective method of conveying consciousness...but it is an ability that can only be used between fairies.

In the long history of fairy civilization, language never manifested. But it was inconvenient to help humans and monsters without any words. Fairies are a far superior species, and it should have been easy to learn the common tongue of the land.

No one anticipated that fairies would be able to learn

language, but not implement it. My language center is not developed enough to convert my advanced thoughts into words.

Hey! What's going on?!

It's not just me. All fairies consider things in a philosophical and high-minded manner, but when converting this into the common tongue of the land, it always comes out in simple terms with a childlike voice. To think that, even with our innate abilities, which are found in no other race, we are so poor at language! To think that our unrivaled strength is simultaneously our weakness! It's infuriating to be considered inferior to other races who must resort to a form of communication as primitive as language, but it doesn't matter.

Without any way to understand my unmanageable aggravation, Lady Sapphee kept touching me. Poking, poking, poking.

"Stop it!" I could only manage a two-syllable objection.

It is our persistent infantile pronunciation that makes other races treat fairies as pets. Even a well-bred lady like Sapphee tends to treat us that way.

I pulled away from her prodding fingers and hopped down to the floor. My landing was perfect. That's what it means to have perfect fairy agility.

"Oh my, I'm sorry."

Even seeing me angry, her attitude was the same as someone who had just teased a small child and thought it was funny that the child was now annoyed. Of course, it hurts my pride when someone as noble as myself is dismissed like this...but Lady Sapphee is still kinder than most people from the other races.

"Well then, let's begin molting." Lady Sapphee announced her most important duty for the day as if nothing had happened. "I will finish before Dr. Glenn arrives. Take your positions."

"Roger that!"

When Lady Sapphee clapped her hands, we all moved. Naturally, I took my post as well, faster than the eye could see. We were not here to waste time being treated as pets.

"Officer! Officer Cottingley!"

"What is it?"

The voice of my wingman Doyle, the adjutant fairy, resounded in my mind. "All teams are in position!"

"Good! What about the entrance to the room?"

"We have complete surveillance. Lumber is in place for backup, and unassailable protection is also in place!"

"Good! Lady Sapphee will begin molting any moment now! Stay alert and perform your duties!"

"Copy!" everyone replied in unison.

As the commander, it is also my job to issue orders. These conversations take only seconds with our innate fairy abilities. I can transmit my voice not only to the adjutant, but to all fairies, even without seeing their faces. This is why there are no fairy messengers. If we wanted to, we could deliver reports to the far away fairy Land of Youth, where the Queen sits on her imperial throne.

Telepathy is so effective, and no other races can mimic it. Mwahaha!

Now then.

Lady Sapphee was already beginning her preparations for

molting in her quarters. The lamia species molts once every two to three months. Lady Sapphee makes sure to hide herself from everyone during that time. Advanced beings such as fairies have no experience with biological phenomena like molting, but it's easy to understand why Lady Sapphee wouldn't want to be seen in that state.

First, if your skin is coming off, then clothing would naturally get in the way. The lady wears light-shielding intimates on her top half but removes and discards her skirt and accessories on her bottom half. I would imagine that she wouldn't want the love of her life and owner of this clinic—Dr. Glenn Litbeit—to see her undressed. Fairies don't love or marry or give birth, but I understand the logic of the lady's emotion.

"Humph."

Loving another... That's something someone like me, a mere commander, will never have to deal with. Fairy reproduction is a special right granted only to the Fairy Queen. The only happiness we other fairies can hope for is to commit ourselves to serving the health and body of the Queen. In other words, we don't need love.

Actually, I don't even consider myself to be a woman.

The difference between the sexes in the fairy species is already quite vague, but it seems that I am especially lacking in femininity—not that it matters, so long as it doesn't affect my duties.

"Umph..."

I heard Lady Sapphee's voice. It seemed she'd begun molting.

"Mmm... Umph... Ahh..."

I stood as tall as I could on a chair in the middle of the room to see what was happening in her living quarters. Lady Sapphee was continuously rubbing her body against the post of her own bed.

"Mmm... Mmm... Ahh..."

This hip motion came easily to lamia. Lady Sapphee had the torso of a human, but her bottom half was lamia. She rubbed the line that divided the top of her body from the bottom against the corner of the post repeatedly.

It wouldn't be long now.

I could hear her surface skin peeling off—starting with the scales on the bottom half of her body—with a soft tearing sound. The molting had begun. Her old lamia skin peeled when the scales were rubbed against something with an edge, like the bedpost.

It was going smoothly.

We had always kept watch when Lady Sapphee was molting. The unique trust in our relationship was built on this duty.

"Mmm... Umph... Ugh..."

Lady Sapphee changed her movements. She began deliberately rubbing the already-peeling skin against the floor. Now and then, she would wiggle her snake belly, and that peristaltic motion would move the skin farther down toward her tail. Before long, the movements became bigger, changing to an exercise that took up the entire room. She ran around the room in circles, sometimes lying face up or on her belly, rubbing the bottom half of her body against the wall and using other movements at varying speeds to move the molting along. She was now panting.

This was certainly a biological phenomenon, but to me, this molting process looked like rigorous fitness training. Lady

Sapphee, out of breath, continued shedding her skin through these violent movements. The old skin peeled off her snake body, coiling up on the floor like a balled-up old sock.

"Mmm! Agh! Umph!"

Even the way Lady Sapphee wriggled her hips was violent. She made large, writhing movements, and the wave-like motion traveled all the way down to the tip of her tail. The lamia method of molting took great effort.

This was another reason why a lamia wouldn't want to be seen molting by a man they were in love with. They would be exposing him to the repeated contortions of their entire body while moaning loudly. Fairies have almost no vulgar emotions—such as libido—whatsoever, but I could still understand this. Lady Sapphee's movements were provocative. She wouldn't want to arouse such lust in the man she loved. Molting was an important matter to the lamia, and it had nothing to do with seduction. It was not flirtatious behavior to show to a gentleman. The promiscuous sounds and movements were unintentional.

"Umph... Mmm, umph... Ahh... Hee..."

Lamia don't sweat, so how do they regulate their body temperature when exercising? That's why Lady Sapphee had prepared a bucket in the room beforehand. Lamia wet the bottom half of their bodies as needed. In this way, they keep their skin and scales moist, maintaining an appropriate humidity that makes the molting process easier. Also, the moisture on their snake half evaporates with an increase in body temperature. When the moisture evaporates, it lowers their body temperature. Then, the water that has evaporated from such a huge body increases the humidity of the room. To us, this looks like a steam bath, but what they are doing is no day at the spa. Lady Sapphee was out of breath, and her cheeks were flushed due to her rising body temperature. My subordinates would also sometimes draw water to wet Lady Sapphee's body.

"Mmm... Argh..."

Lady Sapphee grabbed the bed frame and locked her limbs with her upper body lifted upward. She then wiggled her hips from side to side. She switched from the vertical movements she had been doing to horizontal exercises, trying to get the old skin off. The bottom half of her body undulated from side to side. The way Lady Sapphee's hip movements rippled down her body made it look like she was performing an eccentric dance that I didn't know.

"Oof. Ugh. Ahh. Mmm. Umph." The lady's voice got quicker. Her old skin was already halfway off.

Lady Sapphee's smell filled the humid room. It wasn't unpleasant. Perhaps the faint perfume was the ointment she used to block sunlight. The ointment mixed with the evaporated moisture and filled the room.

"Oof. Mmm. Ahh... Mmm!"

She stretched both arms downward to support her upper body and create a precise friction with the floor using the bottom half of her body. Her heavy breathing made it apparent how hard she was working. The light clothing required for molting; the violently repeated undulating motion; the body moistened to control body temperature and the humid room; the chaotic breathing and voice…

"I wouldn't want to be seen like this, either," one of my subordinates commented. When you have telepathic powers, even your private thoughts are conveyed.

"Private Wright, you are on duty." I reprimanded the fairy directly, as is my duty as commanding officer.

"Y-yes, ma'am. I apologize, Your Excellency."

Incidentally, it seemed Dr. Glenn was on house calls throughout Lindworm and wouldn't be back until the evening. Lady Sapphee must have timed her molting with that in mind.

The thin skin that had peeled off was translucent, but it also appeared to be a faint pink color. This color and texture would change once it had dried out. Conversely, the newly exposed epidermis was a clean, pure white. This brilliant color could only be seen directly after molting, and, with time, it would gradually settle into the pink coloration as well. At least, that was what happened every time Lady Sapphee had molted before. Everything was going smoothly as planned.

"Your Excellency! All clear for each unit!"

"Good. Continue to stand by. Don't let your guard down!"

It was perfect, thankfully. Although, it was getting a bit dull just watching Lady Sapphee's writhing body. Such a waste of an opportunity to show off the talents of a Cottingley. No offense to Lady Sapphee, but I had hoped for some sort of challenge that would put our fairy powers to the test.

"Mmm. Gah. Mmm…"

The molting progressed to the next stage.

Lady Sapphee lifted her hips and planted her upper body against the floor. Holding that position, she made a circle with the tail part of her lower body, looping her tail through the center. She was, in a sense, tying her lower body into a knot. You would have to possess the long lower body of a lamia to tie yourself into a knot in the first place, but Lady Sapphee took it a step further by moving the knot. She wiggled her snake-like body, sliding the knot to the tip of her tail. In addition to the friction with the floor and wall, she was also creating friction with her lower body.

"Mmm... Argh... Mmm!"

As the knot passed the peeling skin, the friction caused the skin to peel away. It really was a wondrous molting trick.

A significant length of skin had already come off. Even so, there were no pieces of skin scattered about. The old skin was intact, maintaining the body's shape. If such a massive exuvia was discovered on a mountain somewhere, whoever found it would think a snake large enough to eat a horse in one bite had shed its skin.

"Your Excellency!"

In the middle of thinking about all this, the adjutant suddenly called me.

"What is it, Doyle?"

"There's a problem! It's... It's hard to say."

"Out with it!"

"Private Wright accidently added a chemical to the bucket of water for controlling her body heat!"

"What?!"

How careless could they be? I would have to train them harder.

There were many chemicals in the clinic used for treatments. It went without saying that those chemicals had to be handled with the utmost caution. Carelessness on the part of my subordinates was ultimately my responsibility. If it were a dangerous chemical, then Lady Sapphee might not emerge unscathed.

"How did this happen?"

"Um... Well, it seems the chemical was Lady Sapphee's personal sample product, and there was no label! The private said he thought it was just water," the adjutant explained.

"Hmph... And what type of chemical was it?"

"It was a love potion made from mandrake."

"What did you say?!" I hadn't realized I was yelling. It is a rare thing for a fairy's thoughts to match with their voice.

A love potion... What an absurd thing to sample! Love potions and aphrodisiacs made from mandrake exerted stronger effects than any other similar potions. Maybe she was planning to use it on Dr. Glenn... *No, don't jump to conclusions.*

Lady Sapphee was a doctor who conducted various types of research. It's possible that she was simply testing the effects of a love potion as part of her research...but she should at least label her experiments!

"Mmm... Ah-ahhh!"

Before I could finish my thought, the lady let out a high-pitched scream. Even I could discern what was happening—she was sexually excited. A fair amount of water had already been applied to her body to control her body temperature. It was only natural that the effects of the mandrake love potion would begin manifesting.

"Doyle, hurry up and draw water from the well. Step up the body temperature control!"

"Roger that!"

Doyle flew out the window, leading Unit 1. The well was just next to the window. Using their fairy strength, they would be able to bring in pure water right away.

Whether from the effects of the love potion or not, Lady Sapphee's cheeks were already flushed. "Mmm. Mph. Mmm... Ahh!"

I wondered what it felt like to shed your own skin. Even though it was old skin, there had to be some stimulation when skin that, up until just before, had been your own scales peeled off. The look on Lady Sapphee's face was one directly between pain and pleasure that couldn't be described with words.

According to Lady Sapphee, when the time for her to molt draws close, her skin gets itchy, so I wondered if there were also some pleasure from that itch sensation going away. Now the effects of the love potion had been added to the mix. I could see her shoulders trembling, possibly from the increased pleasure. Even so, she was still moving her hips, desperately trying to complete her molting.

"Ahh. Hmm. Mmm!"

Before long, Lady Sapphee's movements became steady and rhythmic. She tied her lower body in a knot and moved the knot to the tip of her tail over and over. She swayed her hips widely from side to side to control her movements. Her breathing was becoming more and more rapid.

"Hff! Ahh! Argh... Mmmwaa!"

Her euphoric voice could probably be heard from outside the room. I wondered what might have happened if Dr. Glenn had been in the clinic instead of out on house calls. He and Lady Sapphee lived under the same roof; he would have at least noticed her voice.

Lamia, who can't live without undergoing the biological phenomenon of molting, are an inferior species compared to fairies, but I understand their girlish desire to go through the process without being seen by the man they love.

Most of all, helping to solve the complicated troubles of other races shows our devotion to the Fairy Queen. We noble fairies are not a species that is subordinate to other races. The aid we provide to them is a favor and an act of goodwill. It is because of our superior existence that we must care for the other races.

There is nothing easy about being a fairy.

"Mmmmmm! Mmm! Mmmmmm!"

All at once, Lady Sapphee's voice became louder. She put a hand over her mouth, as if her own voice had surprised her. I'm sure the lady never imagined that she was under the influence of a love potion.

The molting progressed with a slurping sound. The peeling of her skin was not consistent, and, at times, larger parts than others would peel. Her snake tail squirmed at the sensation of the molting, swinging from side to side.

"Aah… Argh. Argh. Aah!"

Lady Sapphee steadied her breathing, taking a short break.

But then the molting resumed all at once. Only about a quarter of the lower body remained. She was almost done.

"Your Excellency! Excellency!" A voice echoed in the back of my brain.

This voice was unmistakably Sergeant Griffith, put in charge of watching over the subordinates. The moment I realized this, I suddenly became tense. The urgency in the voice told me that whatever he was about to report wasn't good.

"What is it now?"

"Dr. Glenn has returned!"

"He's back earlier than planned. What's going on?!"

"We don't know! But it didn't seem like he was in a hurry. It's possible he's just stopping by in the middle of his rounds…"

"Damn." I checked on Lady Sapphee's status.

It looked as though the molting had taken a toll on her, and she was still breathing hard. She had never gotten this excited while molting in the past. The love potion must have had a tremendous impact. She may not be able to move right away, and, even if she had, her clothes were still too revealing to greet the doctor.

"Hurry! Hurry!" (Translation: *Thou art in danger! I request thou act swiftly!*)

"Hurry! You must!" (Translation: *We will make an appropriate judgment call to save thee from the looming danger!*)

My subordinates gathered around Lady Sapphee, each

speaking out to her. Of course, I could understand what they were really saying, but from Lady Sapphee's perspective, we cute little fairies were just making a fuss. At first, I thought we should discuss what measures to take with Lady Sapphee, but I soon vetoed that idea. The way she was staring off into space told me she was not able to make the necessary decisions.

Part of the blame for creating this situation lay with us fairies. *Always choose the optimum solution when fulfilling your duties, Cottingley!*

"Listen up!"

Our innate fairy abilities were working at full capacity. I gave out orders to all fairies under my command.

"I am officially initiating Phase C, due to emergency circumstances! All units, take your positions!"

All my subordinates began moving as soon as I gave the orders.

The biggest inconvenience of this room was the lack of a lock on the door. This breach in security was unacceptable for the quarters of a grown woman. The only way to lock this room would be to bar the door from the inside by wedging a piece of wood in the handle, which we did. At the same time, we stacked more pieces of wood, adding weight so the door wouldn't break. This way, no one, short of a giant, would be able to open the door easily.

"Sapphee?" A voice came from outside. It was Dr. Glenn Litbeit.

According to my observations, he was one of the dumber humans. Certainly, he was skilled in treatment techniques for monsters, and that was one of the reasons the people of this town loved him. But we fairies, who exist in this world by the grace of the Fairy Queen, do not age or change and are rarely injured. Even if we were to injure our bodies, we can recover instantly—so long as we return to the Land of Youth, where we come from, so the Fairy Queen may bestow her power upon us. Without the need to benefit from medical care, we can't effectively evaluate someone just by knowing they are a doctor. Dr. Glenn was absentminded, thick-skinned, and—I have to say it—lacked much when it came to going about daily business smoothly. That was the type of man he was.

"Sapphee, are you there?"

The moment she heard his voice, Lady Sapphee seemed to realize her darling Dr. Glenn had returned home. Her shoulders trembled with fear. He tried opening the door, but thanks to our preparations, there was no way anyone could enter that room from outside.

"Umph. Hey, why is the door closed?"

"Not now!"

Ugh! Now more than ever, on behalf of the lady in distress, I needed to somehow get Dr. Glenn to comprehend the extremely sensitive state of this room! Why couldn't I just say the words? *Lady Saphentite is currently in an indelicate state and cannot be seen. Please return after several hours. I appreciate your gentlemanly conduct.*

"It's impossible!"

The only thing that was impossible was my ability to form words. With only simple words such as these, Dr. Glenn would certainly be left with nothing but suspicion.

"I see..."

Huh?

However, Dr. Glenn did not pursue the issue further. Or perhaps it was that he comprehended something about the situation. He did linger a bit by the door, but he did not try to open it.

"Excellent. Dr. Glenn is not taking action! Francis, monitor him for me in front of the door! If anything happens, report to me immediately!"

"Roger that, Your Excellency!"

"Elsea, take Unit 2 and maintain surveillance over each post!"

"Yes, sir!"

"That's 'ma'am' to you!"

I didn't particularly mind being treated like a man, but that was taking it too far!

After I gave my orders, I rushed back to Lady Sapphee's side, perfectly demonstrating the speed of my lightweight form. I saw the deflection in her eyes. She hadn't expected Dr. Glenn to come back at this time. If he had somehow gotten into the room, he would have seen her half-naked, immodest form. It would have been easier to just tell him honestly that she was molting. But it was probably embarrassing for lamia to have their molting and egg-laying cycles known by others. It may be considered equivalent to a human woman's menstruation cycle being discovered. It was something a fairy like me would never understand.

I hopped up onto Lady Sapphee's shoulder and whispered in her ear. "Hurry! Quickly!"

Why was it that my voice could be so relaxed without any

sense of urgency? It was vexing that this voice was coming from my own mouth, but all I could do was believe that my thoughts were being conveyed properly to Lady Sapphee.

"Mmm… I-I know." Lady Sapphee wasn't paying complete attention. She began rubbing the end of her tail against the floor. However, perhaps because of the stimulation of the molting up to that point, her movements were awkward.

Hmm.

If it were possible, I would have peeled off the old skin for her, but if hands as small as ours were to touch the skin, it would tear into tiny pieces instead of the nice, clean single piece that was already coming off. That would be pointless. The other goal with this molting was to create a single, uncut exuvia.

"Mmm… Ahh… Argh… Ugh!"

"Don't rush it!"

"I can't help it!"

Normally, Lady Sapphee would have maintained a composed expression, saying something like, "I would never mix business and pleasure with Dr. Glenn," but she was in a state of crisis. This was a rare moment of desperation for her.

"Doyle!"

When I called his name, my prudent adjutant replied immediately.

"Yes, Your Excellency?"

"Prepare for Phase D!"

"Right! Change of clothes and all other preparations are already in place!" Doyle replied.

"Good. Make sure everything is finished before Dr. Glenn comes in!"

"Roger! Everything will be completely cleaned up!"

I could always count on my adjutant, Doyle. He was my most trusted subordinate.

The fairies' work would begin once the molting was complete, but Lady Sapphee would have to make the final push before we could move on to that step.

"Mmm… Hmph… Mmmmmm!"

Lady Sapphee was working hard to remove the last bit of skin, rubbing her tail on the floor. But for some reason, that last push wasn't going well. If she could just peel off a little bit more, it would all come off. Lady Sapphee was used to this, so why was she having so much trouble this time?

Oh… Dr. Glenn.

The presence of the man she loved was making the normally competent Lady Sapphee tremble.

"Sapphee?"

"Hmm?! Ha! Argh?!"

Ugh!

After we'd made it this far, Dr. Glenn was calling from the other side of the door. Son of a… He couldn't have had worse timing. *Why can't you just shut up and wait?!* To be called by the man she loved while still under the influence of the love potion… Lady Sapphee looked like she was in a state of panic.

"I can hear your voice… Are you all right?"

"F-fine… I'm fine!"

"Are you sure? You don't sound fine..."

"I-I'm fine... Mmm... mmm. Uh, ah, just wait... Just wait for a few minutes... Please!"

"But—"

"Sometimes women need time to get ready!"

Once Sapphee said that, my subordinates jumped in.

"Yeah, yeah!"

"The manly thing to do is wait!"

"Where is your sensitivity?!"

Without waiting for my orders, my subordinates laid into Glenn. See how much Lady Sapphee was loved and respected by them?

"I-I see."

"That's right! That's right!"

Dr. Glenn grasped the unusual ambiance in the room and stopped talking. Lady Sapphee seized her opportunity and went back to her tail molting. She covered her mouth with both hands so she wouldn't cry out and moved the lower half of her body using only her waist, desperately trying to shed her old skin.

"Mmmph! Mm! Mmm!"

I wondered what Dr. Glenn could be thinking. It was easy to tell she was muffling her voice through the thin exam room door.

I wanted to explain to Lady Sapphee that molting was nothing to be ashamed of, but, well...with my limited language abilities, I would only be misunderstood. All I could do was pray that Dr. Glenn would at least understand Lady Sapphee's girlish feelings.

"Mmmmmm! Mmmph!"

Lady Sapphee was feeling both shame and passion. I'm sure she was feeling a variety of other emotions as well, as she swayed with an expression of desperation on her face. She couldn't even take her time to make sure the skin didn't tear. She was just trying to finish the task without raising her voice. It would be impossible for Dr. Glenn to fully comprehend. They were both still young, and they weren't the type of people who could be together without any hitches in the relationship. There was no helping it.

But I, Cottingley Bradford VI, would do everything in my power to help.

"You can do it!" I whispered words of encouragement in Lady Sapphee's ear.

What a dumb thing to say. But I hoped those simple words would convey to Lady Sapphee my high-minded thoughts and the prayers in my heart. This was the only way a fairy, superior to other species, could convey encouragement. This encouragement had nothing to do with the Great Fairy Queen. It was coming from me, Cottingley.

The last of the skin slipped off.

"Umph. Finally!"

I saw Lady Sapphee smile joyfully. I immediately gave orders to my subordinates.

"Excellent! Initiate Phase D! All units together now!"

With Adjutant Doyle at the forefront, my subordinates replied.

"Right!"

"Roger!"

"Yes, ma'am!"

Some of them put the nurse uniform we had prepared onto Lady Sapphee. Others fixed the furniture left in disarray from when the lady was moving around the room. She had been writhing around so much that it looked as if the room had been burglarized, but it only took a moment for the space to return to its original, orderly state. The exuvia was quickly put into a cloth bag that we had prepared and hidden away in the closet. Normally it was also our job to dispose of the exuvia, but, for some reason, this time Lady Sapphee said she wanted to save it. We didn't know the reason, but we succeeded in storing it without a scratch.

"Clothes are on!"

"The room is in order!"

"We also hid the exuvia. It won't be found, Your Excellency!"

"Good! Now open the door! Once Dr. Glenn has entered the room, all units out!"

"Roger!"

Everyone removed the wooden pieces holding the door shut and hid them under the bed. Phase D was the final step of today's duties as well as an extremely important camouflage so Dr. Glenn would have no idea what Lady Sapphee had been doing. Once we succeeded in this, our task would be complete, and we would be free to return to our normal duties.

"You can come in now, Doctor."

I stowed away in the closet with the exuvia and monitored the room through the crack in the door.

"Y-yes... Um, what happened?"

"It was nothing important."

I thought Lady Sapphee was still breathing hard. But maybe I only noticed because I had witnessed the entire molting ordeal. Without that knowledge, perhaps it would only seem like she was rushing to get herself ready.

"Let's put that aside. Doctor, I thought you were going to be making rounds today."

"Yes, I have to go out again soon. I just thought I would have some lunch. I bought some sandwiches at the stall on the main road. Would you join me?!"

"Why, Doctor, aren't you thoughtful!"

That was Dr. Glenn. He picked the worst times to be thoughtful. If he would just show that much consideration normally, then I'm sure Lady Sapphee wouldn't be so anxious!

"Also...I heard a strange rumor, and I wanted to check on you."

"Strange rumor?"

"Someone said they saw you on the street... They tried calling your name, but said you ignored them."

"What?"

That was strange. Lady Sapphee rarely went out unless it was absolutely necessary. Furthermore, she had stayed in her room to molt today, so no one would have seen her outside.

"I didn't think you would have gone out for any reason, but I came back to check, just in case."

"I've been in my room this whole time."

"Well, I guess it must have been a doppelgänger..."

A doppelgänger. I had heard a similar rumor. Fairies love rumors. Like, meeting yourself, or the phenomenon of encountering someone in a place where they would never be. In other words, a rumor created by your eyes playing tricks on you...or a hallucination. Some say there are ghosts and spirits that create illusions, so it could have been that. There was also a time when fairies deliberately confused humans by using enchantments.

"That seems to be happening so much lately," said Lady Sapphee. "I mean, seeing someone in a place where they aren't."

"There's a rumor of that going around Lindworm."

"So...now someone has seen *my* doppelgänger?"

Dr. Glenn nodded. It must have worried him, causing him to rush back. Actually, there was an even *more* sinister rumor having to do with the doppelgängers. It's said that if you saw your own doppelgänger, you would die soon. The rumors had spread so quickly because of *that* frightening addition to the story.

It was absurd.

Monsters like doppelgängers don't exist. It is either a case of mistaken identity, or a trick being played by someone. People don't die from mistaken identity. Of course, it's possible that a ghost could show you a vision then suck the living spirit out of you—but there are no beings in Lindworm that would commit such violence. As a doctor, Glenn had to know that there had never been a case of a doppelgänger causing death. I couldn't believe he would be misled by such a ridiculous rumor. But I understood why he would be worried for Lady Sapphee.

"Well, thank goodness it's nothing. Let's eat."

"Yes, Doctor."

"I can wait if you want to clean up from your molting first, though."

"Huh?!" Lady Sapphee opened her eyes wide, and her face turned bright red.

He noticed?! There was no way. We fairies covered it up perfectly! And even if he did somehow find out, why would he say it like that?! The simpleton! But then, how would Dr. Glenn understand a lady's feelings? He was like an idiotic teenager, and his entire clinic would fall apart if there were no fairies to run things.

"D-Doctor, you knew?! The whole time?"

"No, I had no idea until I came into the room. But I knew the moment I saw you."

"What?"

"Your scales are shiny. I know that's what you look like when you've just molted."

At that, Lady Sapphee finally looked at the lower part of her body. Her scales were white and shiny, slick like silk, and completely unblemished. That was the beauty of lamia scales.

"Oh... Um, well..."

"They're beautiful, your new scales."

"Oh?!"

"I'll be waiting downstairs."

Dr. Glenn! He just says whatever he wants then runs away?! That's how he acts after toying with a young woman?! I can't just sit around and watch this without saying anything!

That's what I was thinking anyway, but, in the end, my complaints went unheard by Dr. Glenn. My words would be wasted on a species that could only communicate their feelings through the inconvenient mode of language.

I just sat there, livid.

That's when Lady Sapphee opened the closet door. Her face was still red. Of course it was. Dr. Glenn hadn't noticed our presence, but Lady Sapphee had lost face by having her secret—which we had worked so hard to keep—pointed out.

Hmm.

Those were my first thoughts, but when I looked closer, Lady Sapphee's face was relaxed. Perhaps it's because the fairy species is far superior to any other race, but humans and monsters say that our expressions are difficult to read. For us, unless it's a face we're very familiar with, the faces of non-fairy beings all look the same.

Even so, I understood her expression. Lady Sapphee was clearly, desperately trying to smile.

"Dr. Glenn figured it out, even with all the help from the fairies..."

"Sapphee, are you happy?"

"Happy?! Don't think for a second that I'm suddenly smitten just because Dr. Glenn is paying attention to me! I may be slightly pleased that he complimented my scales—but that's all."

Although her tail did seem to be flapping quite a bit.

I take back what I said about Dr. Glenn being insensitive. He pays closer attention to the bodies of monsters than you would expect. Perhaps he was looking at her more with the mind of a physician, like an occupational disorder, rather than as a woman. But that shouldn't have mattered to Lady Sapphee.

How pathetic! I'm not here to get carried away by the intimacies of lovers.

"Sapphee—"

"Yes?"

"I'm sorry."

My subordinates and I all humbled ourselves. This was about the love potion. However, Lady Sapphee tilted her head to the side, puzzled. Perhaps she hadn't noticed. I wanted to explain my subordinate's blunder and the effects of the love potion we had discovered in detail, but I didn't have the confidence to explain it in a way Lady Sapphee would understand.

Lady Sapphee stroked my head with her index finger. It was disrespectful, but she probably meant it to indicate acceptance of my apology. I swallowed my pride and resigned myself to her fingertip.

"What about this?" I asked.

"Yes, that exuvia. There is a frame in the warehouse. Will you put it inside and display it for me? The frame might be too small, but if it is, you can cut the exuvia."

An odd request. But there was no reason to refuse. My subordinates and I got to moving again. First, we needed to carry the exuvia to the warehouse. My subordinates picked up the cloth bag that held it. It was a large load for fairies, but with our teamwork, nothing could hold us back.

"You really saved me today. I mean, you always save me, but today especially. I wish I could increase your pay, but... Well, you wouldn't hear of it, would you?"

"No way!"

The remuneration for using fairies was one bowl of milk per person. However, this was not a demand that fairies made because they loved milk. It was because the Fairy Queen gloried in our labor—which served both humans and monsters—for a flat fee. It would never do to change our fee based on the work done.

"Well, the same amount of milk as always then. I will go downstairs to have my lunch."

"Good work! Have fun!"

Lady Sapphee smiled like a blooming flower and went downstairs.

I am Cottingley Bradford VI. Regardless of species, or whether I am praised or disparaged, so long as I am paid, I will perform my job, putting my personal feelings aside. Even if my feelings go unheard, even if my thoughts are simplified into speech, I will not object. We do not serve so that we may receive praise. We accomplish what we must, regardless of whether we are admired. We are the mighty fairies. Everything we do is for the Fairy Queen.

But, well... I can't say that I disliked seeing Lady Sapphee's smile of relief and gratitude. I think the Fairy Queen would forgive me for taking that as encouragement in my endeavors.

"What are your orders, Your Excellency?!" my courageous subordinates spoke in unison. We were a veteran corps.

It wasn't Dr. Glenn or Lady Sapphee preserving the peace and order in this clinic. It was the highest order of fairies, led by me, Cottingley.

"Okay! Everyone! Our mission is almost complete! Don't let your guard down until the job is done!"

"Right!" they spoke in unison again.

"But I can't overlook the issue of the love potion! Ten laps around the room for everyone before we continue the mission!"

"What?!"

"No complaints! Everyone is responsible!"

At that, my subordinates began running.

The famous story of the elves and the shoemaker is not simply a tale. We are just here trying to fulfill our duties. Not as figments of your imagination, but as real, live fairies. Sooner or later, all other races will bow to the fairies!

I can't wait until that happens. *Mwahahaha!*

"Mwahahaha!"

Even with my meager language ability as a fairy, my loud laugh came out precisely as I meant it to.

CASE 02:
The Centaur with a Bruise

TISALIA SCYTHIA, the centaur princess, was an early riser.

She rose from her bed—a luxurious, canopied affair, large enough for a centaur to lie down upon—at the break of dawn. Thanks to the achievements of Scythia Transportation, Tisalia, heir to the company, was able to live extravagantly.

"Ahhh..."

It was a sleepy morning. Tisalia stifled a yawn as she pulled herself out of bed. Two attendants, Kay and Lorna, awaited her. It was their job to wake up earlier than their employer. Tisalia's morning ritual included wiping her face with a cloth, fixing her hair, and changing clothes. As the trueborn daughter of the house, Tisalia's morning preparations were all performed by her attendants. But she kept it simple: Her hair was tied back, out of the way, and over her undergarments, she wore a cotton sweatshirt. That was the extent of it.

Once she was ready, she left the room with Kay and Lorna.

The hallway was wide enough for several centaurs to walk abreast. They passed through the hall to the foyer and outside to the yard, where an especially tall centaur waited for them.

He was just past fifty years old, his expression stern under his mustache. He was bare-chested, muscular, and swinging a practice sword. A pool of sweat had formed on the ground around him, suggesting he had already been training for a significant amount of time that morning. Here was a veteran warrior who looked like he could take on a giant if the situation called for it. A closer look at his bare torso revealed multiple scars.

"Umph." When the man saw Tisalia come out into the garden, he stopped swinging the sword.

"Good morning, Father."

"Yeah." Tisalia's father, Hephthal, head of Scythia Transportation, gave a generous nod.

"I'm going to take my morning run."

"Fine. Be careful." Hephthal grinned.

If you only saw his smile, he may have seemed like a soft-spoken gentleman having a conversation with his daughter. But Tisalia could easily imagine him wearing the same smile while wielding a sword as long as he was tall and attacking an enemy camp.

"Kay, Lorna, take care of my daughter."

"Yes, master."

"Leave everything to us."

Her father worried too much… At least, that's what Tisalia thought. But she couldn't say such a thing.

Tisalia felt pure joy whenever she trained with Kay and Lorna. For that reason, she always gave her all with her attendants.

"Heh." She smiled despite herself. Behind her father's swinging motions, the male employees were practicing under the instruction of the chief steward.

A sharp sound came from yet another direction. Tisalia looked over to see her mother cutting straw with a halberd. Her mother must have been feeling good that day, since she had brought out a real weapon. But Tisalia didn't see the maids who were always by her mother's side. If they weren't in the yard, then perhaps they were meditating in the bathhouse.

The sight of centaurs lined up in training had to be quite a spectacle if you weren't used to it. But such was the mansion where Tisalia Scythia lived.

The Scythia clan ran a transportation company these days, but they had originally been mercenaries. Only those employees who were strong and whose skills were recognized by Hephthal—the head of the family—were allowed to live in the mansion. Many had participated in the war ten years prior, and they never missed a morning training session.

Of course, Scythia Transportation's business was expanding significantly now. They had recently added other species, such as harpies, for delivery of letters and small packages, and cyclops, who dealt in automobile maintenance, to the payroll. So this group wasn't representative of the entire company.

"Kay, have you heard this joke?"

"Huh?"

"The other day, a burglar broke into the guardroom of a certain mansion. He went on and on about how he had come to steal things and screamed, 'Arrest me!' But he hadn't stolen anything, not a single jewel. Do you know why?"

"Umm..." Kay cocked her head to the side.

Lorna answered for her instead. "It was because he broke into *this* mansion, right?"

"Yes. But once he broke in, even the maids and butlers looked tough! The attendants serving as security were the powerful Scythia! There were tons of expensive weapons and armor, not to mention the art and decorations, but he didn't even notice any of them! He freaked out all on his own and ran away, then asked the guards to take him into custody!" Tisalia laughed out loud.

She would be telling this story at parties for a while. It was even funnier because it was true. On account of the owner transitioning from the mercenary business to the transport business, the employees were all skilled in martial arts. Well, that wasn't quite true; it would be an exaggeration to say that *all* the household effects were weapons. Nevertheless, this was Tisalia's home. It was the residence of a clan so famous for their strength that even burglars ran away, barefoot.

Morning training was a daily task for Tisalia. Her training was merciless—as one would expect of a warrior. And even though Tisalia was known as the centaur princess, there wasn't a trace of princess-like elegance when she trained.

She started with an early morning run.

She ran through Lindworm's main road. She galloped to the central square and back without stopping—her normal route. In the early morning, the roads were empty. Since she didn't have to worry about an accident, she could run at full speed.

During this particular morning run, Tisalia saw Illy flying in the air, delivering newspapers. Illy served as a subcontractor from the harpy village, but she had already grown used to her role in sky delivery.

After her run, Tisalia returned to the mansion yard and began her weapons training with Kay and Lorna.

"Umph!"

"Atta!"

"Yaaah!"

Kay was acting as her opponent today. Lorna played the role of referee. Tisalia and Kay bellowed battle cries and crossed their practice swords. Even before the sweat from her morning run had dried, Tisalia was sweating anew from the swordplay. Centaurs had huge bodies, which called for great amounts of exercise and led to a large volume of sweat. This was exacerbated by their merciless training.

After the first round of weapons training, Tisalia went to the bathhouse. Her bath began with hot water running over her head. Then it was time to cleanse her body. This was also the job of her two attendants, as Tisalia just stood there. Cold drinking water was available in the bathhouse, and she gulped it down. In the summer, the water was prepared with lemon and salt. The attendants also drank their fill.

Once all the sweat had been rinsed from her body, the attendants dried her off, and she left the bathhouse.

Tisalia sat in front of the mirror in the dressing room. This was when she would get ready for the day and make herself presentable to others. Her hair was fixed nicely atop her head, and she wore just a hint of makeup. While warriors had to fight, it was also a glorious profession to the public eye. She couldn't just go without prettying herself up.

Tisalia rose so early every morning because of how much she had to do—from training to making herself presentable. It takes time for a princess to get ready.

With Kay and Lorna's help, her morning tasks were complete.

Next, she moved to the dining hall.

When Tisalia entered the dining hall, her parents were already seated. No matter how busy they were, the family of three always sat down for breakfast together. That was Tisalia's father's policy.

"Sorry I'm late, Father, Mother."

"Well then." Tisalia's father was the head of the company and the glue that held the clan together. No matter how busy he was—all day, every day—with work, he never missed breakfast.

Her father was no longer bare-chested, as he had been during training. He was now in a three-piece suit, the scars from his days as a mercenary hidden beneath his formal attire. He would be managing Lindworm's transportation industry again today.

"Let's eat then. We received a large delivery of tomatoes from Aluloona today. They're in season now and absolutely delicious."

"Yes, they're wonderfully juicy," her mother joined in.

Tisalia picked up her silverware. She enjoyed these moments with her family.

Centaurs were generally vegetarians. This morning's meal included a salad featuring the tomatoes from Aluloona, cornbread, and a soup made from root vegetables. All meals eaten in the mansion were prepared by their contracted chef, so Tisalia never worried about what was in the food.

Biscuits served as garnish for the meal. However, these biscuits were extremely high in salt content. Due to their excessive exercise, centaurs needed that extra sodium. There was no salt to be harvested in Lindworm, but they could get sea salt from the human realm or rock salt from the monster realm, and they did.

"Lorna, today's biscuits are delicious!" Tisalia praised Lorna, who stood by her side, this time serving as a waiter.

Lorna had made the salt biscuits herself. She made them because they were Tisalia's favorite, but Tisalia's parents were also reaching for them. Lorna, who was quite good in the kitchen, let out a modest giggle.

"It's an honor, my lady."

Once the main dish had been consumed, the family enjoyed cups of herbal tea. During meals, family conversations were light and happy, but these moments weren't always just fun and games to Tisalia.

"I almost forgot," Hephthal suddenly perked up, remembering something.

This is it... Tisalia braced herself.

The atmosphere at the table was suddenly tense. Tisalia's father constantly tested her on her capabilities as the heir.

"Today is your promotion examination, right?"

"Yes, Father," Tisalia nodded. She had been expecting this conversation.

"I hear you've already won three in a row. So, how about it? Kay, Lorna, what do you think?"

"Yes, master. This morning, the lady defeated me with ease."

"The lady is full of energy and in high spirits. I am sure she will be promoted."

Her father nodded, listening to Kay and Lorna. "If you win, then you'll have reached the second rank. Make sure you succeed."

Tisalia nodded meekly. "I will make you proud, Father."

When playing the role of daughter in this house, Tisalia wasn't in a commanding position. As a daughter, she was capable, obedient, and a proud member of her department.

The promotion examination took place in the arena, where fighters were separated into seven ranks based on their ability. To ensure an interesting match, and to keep the fights from becoming one-sided, fighters fought with others of the same rank. Rookies started at rank seven, the lowest, and moved up based on their results. The strongest fighters, who'd reached rank one, were the heroes of the arena. Those strong enough to win consecutively at rank one were publicly admitted into the hall of fame. When a hall of famer finally withdrew from fighting, their name was carved into the arena monument, preserving their honor for the ages.

Tisalia had her eye on the hall of fame.

Arena-ranking promotion was important. Selections were made based on the promotion examinations that took place in spring and autumn. Only fighters deemed likely to advance battled against each other. Only those who won four times in a row could be promoted to the next rank. Of course, sometimes, certain fighters who were clearly stronger than others were promoted with special speed—such as Kunai Zenow, who rose to rank one in less than six months.

"The lady has already won three matches," said Kay.

"If she wins today, the news will spread all over Lindworm that she is now a rank-two fighter," Lorna added.

"And I will be a proud father. Tisalia, don't let your guard down."

Tisalia dropped her head. She never let her guard down. She had been on fire for the past six months. She had won match after match and earned her spot as a candidate to be promoted. She couldn't let this opportunity go to waste. She had to win.

She took a drink of her herbal tea to keep herself from getting worked up. If she were to make rank two, she would suddenly reach a new level of fame. People would bet on her matches, there would be a new level of excitement, and there would be more spectators. Tickets would be hard to come by. She would be the flower of the arena.

Even if she never made it to rank one, which was populated by only heroes and monsters, rank two was still a considerable honor.

She would acquire an appropriate amount of fame as the daughter of Scythia, and if—only *if*—she could win today, on the way home, she could stop by the clinic.

He would be there...

"Anyway." This time, it was her mother who spoke. She narrowed her eyes at Tisalia as she drank her herbal tea and ate her biscuits.

Meeting Tisalia's father's expectations wasn't difficult. She had always been a strong and skilled daughter, just as her father expected of her. The problem was her mother. Her father was the type to attack head-on. Her mother, on the other hand, planned schemes *before* going in for the attack.

"How did your marriage interview go, Tisalia? With the gentleman I arranged for you?"

"Madam..."

"Perhaps such a weak prospect is not appropriate for the lady."

"Kay and Lorna, you will hold your tongues. This is an heir issue. You're out of line speaking on this matter."

"Er—" Kay and Lorna became silent. They were powerless when Tisalia's mother took the offensive.

Her mother was about to turn forty, but she looked much younger. Perhaps daily training preserved her youthful looks. She was also active in the company's business, assisting her husband and serving as the fabric holding Scythia Transportation together. But that was business...

For some reason, when she spoke to Tisalia, she became a mother who could speak of nothing but marriage. Tisalia's mother was the only one who ever brought up the subject. She wanted to see her daughter married. She wanted grandchildren as soon as possible.

"Mother, you don't need to set up any more interviews. I already have someone in mind."

"Well, if that's the case, then bring him here. I assume you mean Dr. Glenn from the clinic." Her mother's reply was curt.

If it were so easy, then Tisalia would have already brought him to the mansion.

"Dr. Glenn... Well, he's very busy."

"Hmph. Falling in love with a weak human man. Are you sure you're in the right mind? You are the daughter of the house of Scythia. You need a powerful suitor from your own species."

"Er..." Tisalia felt her face getting hot.

If only her mother could catch a cold, just the once. Then she could visit the clinic and see with her own eyes what a man the doctor was. But her mother was someone who meditated in cold water in the middle of winter. She never so much as sneezed. What could Tisalia do? She could try to find a way to send her mother to the hospital herself... At this point, it was possible she had trained enough to defeat her mother with the spear.

Tisalia let her anger stew as she looked at her mother.

"Don't look at me like that. If you have something to say, then say it."

Tisalia saw the fighting spirit in her mother's eyes. Her mother was just as ready to fight as she was. In the end, they were a family of warriors. The only way they knew how to settle things was with weapons. Come to think of it, it had been quite a while since Tisalia had faced her mother…

"Enough." Her father interrupted the staring contest between mother and daughter with a single word, just before the explosion. "We are eating."

"But, honey…"

"She can only take so much, Kimmeria. And any man who is going to marry into this family should be stronger than our daughter. When you were young, I seem to remember you were saying something along the lines of, 'I'll never marry a man weaker than me!'"

"Er… H-honey! We certainly don't need to talk about when I was young… Not here!" Kimmeria's face turned bright red, and she fell silent.

Tisalia's father had been heir to the Scythia military family, and her mother was from another noble centaur family. Tisalia was eternally interested in that love story. Meanwhile, Kay and Lorna were stifling their laughter at the thought of Tisalia's mother as a young and unruly horse.

But when it came to martial arts, Glenn knew nothing. No one could possibly mistake him for being stronger than Tisalia. If her father knew that, then he'd probably be even more against the match than her mother. Tisalia wasn't sure how strong Glenn was mentally, but it wasn't as if her parents would understand such a thing anyway.

"Well then, Father, I should get going."

"Oh, yes. Kimmeria and I have company business to tend to,

so we won't be able to make it, but I'll be waiting for good news. Give them a fight worthy of our name!"

"Yes, Father."

Tisalia got up quickly from the table. Kay and Lorna followed her.

It wasn't a lie that it was time to head to the arena, but it was also true that Tisalia wanted to get away from her mother's marriage interview attack as soon as possible. Hephthal may have been against this particular suitor because he was weak, but even he was on the side of speeding up Tisalia's marriage talks.

"It's just..." She didn't need this right before such an important match.

Tisalia couldn't stop thinking about Glenn.

It was a fierce battle.

She knew because the cheers didn't cease even after the match was over.

"Ahh... Ahh..."

Tisalia's shoulders moved up and down as she breathed heavily. She was hot and sweating inside her body armor. Her final opponent, Marone Golghar—known as the Green Wind—was a mid-level fighter whom Tisalia had battled many times. Marone had good results, and thus had been selected for the promotion examination. They both had three consecutive wins, so this would be their last battle for the test.

Marone's speed and accuracy had improved from what Tisalia remembered. She smoothly dodged Tisalia's charge and aimed for the gap in her armor with the practice sword.

"Ugh..."

Her arm still hurt.

Marone was mixing in joint-lock techniques. Tisalia had been worried when Marone got hold of her arm, but she had been able to pull away with her natural physical strength and stab her with the spear the moment Marone was off balance.

"My Lady! My Lady!"

"You're winning! You're doing it!"

Kay and Lorna's voices were audible above the crowd. The two normally graceful women were now grinning from ear to ear and clapping their hands.

"My Lady!"

"Princess!"

"You got this!"

Others from Scythia Transportation were also yelling "Princess! Princess!" almost too loudly. Illy was bouncing up and down and looked as if she would fly away. She had stopped by in the middle of her shift just to have a quick look.

Tisalia had...won? It hadn't quite set in yet.

Marone, who had fallen, was being carried off by the arena staff. She was one of the tough lizardfolk, so she probably hadn't been hurt badly, but Tisalia was still a bit worried.

"Ahh... Oof..."

Tisalia couldn't lift the arm that held her spear. Instead, she lifted her right arm high in a sign of victory to the spectators. That's when it happened.

"Amazing! It was just amazing!"

She heard a cool voice that sounded like a bell. But for some reason, that single, nonchalant comment silenced the entire booming arena.

"It could have gone either way. It was fierce. You should be proud, it was a great fight."

A shadow fell across Tisalia.

It was Skadi Dragenfelt.

She must have flown down to the arena floor from the highest terrace seat. The promotion battles were important matches, so members of the Lindworm City Council often attended, but Tisalia never would have thought the head of the council would attend in person. Skadi was recovering from a major surgery that had had Lindworm up in arms and had just resumed her governmental duties. She had already removed her veil, and her cherubic face was visible.

"Th-thank you very much..."

"Yes, well, I'm bored of being a spectator by now."

"Wh-what?"

Skadi's bodyguard was yelling something from the terrace. It was too far to hear, but Tisalia could read her lips: *Run away, now!*

"Tisalia, how about a match?"

"W-with me?"

"It would certainly be exciting."

For the first time ever, Skadi removed her robe in public, showing that she had completely recovered from her illness. She tossed the robe away, revealing the perfectly-fitted inner garments she was wearing. They were probably made of special fabrics from Loose Silk Sewing. They ensured easy movement without her wings and scales getting in the way. She had probably selected these clothes intentionally to make a scene.

"I'm often misunderstood. The truth is that I hate war, but I'm not opposed to a good battle."

There was an uproar in the crowd. Why wouldn't there be? Such a battle wouldn't be a sanctioned event, but it was a rare opportunity to see a dragon fight. And this was Skadi Dragenfelt. Years ago, she'd participated in an exhibition match with the fighters on a whim, but, to make a long story short, she was so far out of their league that all the challengers were beaten out of their senses. Thereafter, Skadi was banned from all fights, including exhibition matches, setting the precedent that someone could be banned without ever even becoming a fighter. The dragoness was legendary at the arena, so much so that she had been given the moniker "Draconess."

There was no question that Tisalia would never be able to take her on.

"Don't worry, I'll go easy on you." Skadi cocked her head to the side as if to ask, *"Why the hesitation?"* But, of course, when your opponent was a dragon, even if they were to pull their punches...the fight could be deadly.

"Er." Tisalia glanced over at the official guest seating. Kay held up her arms in the shape of an X, and Lorna's eyes were cast down as she shook her head vigorously. They were telling her that she needn't take on this fight. Once the referee signaled that the match was over, that was it. Permission had not been granted for Skadi's fight, so no matter how much the Draconess might complain, the fight was over.

But...

The crowd is in an uproar...

The cheers weren't stopping.

After the titillating promotion match between Tisalia and Marone, in which Tisalia had been victorious, the strongest dragon in Lindworm had intruded, challenging the winner. This was the ultimate drama. It was only natural that the crowd would grow excited at such a surprise.

I am a warrior... Putting on a good fight and showing off my skills is my...

The hand that held her spear was shaking.

Tisalia was covered in wounds. Her right arm was hurt, and she was breathing hard. All she wanted to do was go home and get in the bath with an ice-cold fruit drink. But...

"How can I refuse? I accept your challenge. Let's go, Draconess!"

Tisalia fixed her grip on the spear with her shaking hand and charged.

Her opponent may have been a dragon, but she looked like nothing more than a child. She had just recovered from an illness; Tisalia could find an advantage somewhere.

"Typical." Skadi grinned.

"Ha!" Tisalia kicked the ground of the arena and broke into a gallop.

She still had a grip on her spear. She closed the distance between her and the dragon in an instant and prepared to deal a charging blow.

"Too slow."

Skadi easily grabbed the tip of the spear with what felt like enough strength to crush it. Where did she hide all that power in such a tiny body?

"Did you think you could win just by surprising me?"

"No?" Tisalia smiled just a little. She let go of the spear.

"Eh?" Skadi was caught off guard and lost her balance.

"That was poor form! I'm sorry!" With her body free after letting go of the spear, Tisalia lifted her forelegs high into the air. She adjusted slightly and took aim...

Then she brought her hooves down Skadi while she was vulnerable, using her entire bodyweight.

"Oof!"

"Argh!"

This move was called the hoof drop. Tisalia figured it was the only way she could possibly cause any damage to an opponent as fierce as Skadi. The move was prohibited in normal matches. Depending on where you hit, it had the potential to crush internal organs or shatter bones. If someone were to kill their opponent, their reputation as a fighter would come into question. But Tisalia was sure that Skadi would be able to take a hoof drop without dying.

"You're...good."

That's when Tisalia realized that she had been too optimistic. Skadi dodged Tisalia's hoof drop with extraordinary reflexes. Tisalia, spear-less, fell to the ground. It seemed like the situation had been reversed. But Tisalia still had a trick up her sleeve.

Now!

There'd been resistance when she touched Skadi's shoulder. She hadn't been able to crush Skadi with her hooves, but she must have caused some damage. She picked up her spear and chased after Skadi.

"That's it, Centaur Princess. I'm just getting started..." Skadi opened her palm to grab the spear again. "I said I'd go easy on you."

Moments later, Tisalia's world flipped upside down.

× × ✖ × ×

"What the hell were you thinking?"

"You had already been promoted!"

"How many times are you going to say it? Sometimes a woman has to stand up for herself!"

"My Lady, that's every time with you."

"You need to learn when to withdraw from a fight."

"Ugh. I know! I'm just stubborn!"

In the end, Tisalia had succumbed to Skadi's counterattack.

She hurt all over. She had already been battered from her fight with Marone, and on top of that were the new injuries from her encounter with Skadi. Her entire body was bruised and aching.

Skadi's tactics were mainly composed of throwing moves. She'd eluded Tisalia's charge, grabbed the spear, and thrown her.

"I thought she said she'd go easy on me..."

Tisalia saw through Skadi. Tisalia's opening attack—the hoof drop—had caught Skadi completely off guard. Whether it was because she had just recovered from her illness, or because it had been too long since she last fought, it didn't matter. She had let her guard down.

If Tisalia had only nailed the hoof drop, she probably would have won. Of course, she hadn't nailed it because of the difference in their speed.

After that, Skadi threw Tisalia over and over, almost as if in revenge. Once she was in her groove, there was no stopping her. Was it an Aiki move? Whatever it was, Tisalia didn't have the means to respond to it.

Using Kay and Lorna's shoulders to prop herself up, Tisalia headed toward the arena medical office. She was just able to walk, so she didn't need a stretcher—but, in any case, she had to get checked out. The arena doctor only specialized in humans. He did examine monsters in emergency cases, but patients with severe injuries were transported to the Central Hospital. The doctor was also passionate about examining human fighters, but was careless when it came to monsters, perhaps because it wasn't his specialty.

It would be so much better if the doctor knew about monsters... Like Glenn.

"I've been waiting for you, Tisalia."

Tisalia's eyes opened wide at the sound of that voice. "Wha... D-Doctor?!"

"Yes, please have a seat. It seems you've suffered a full-body contusion. Let me make sure you don't have any broken bones."

"Er... Um..."

How? Why? She was trembling too much to articulate her question. She didn't know why Glenn Litbeit was in the arena medical office. Of course, she had no qualms about being examined by Glenn.

"You know, I was trying to imagine what it could be when the arena staff burst into my clinic. I had heard there someone was fighting with Skadi, so I knew there would be injuries. I hurried over as fast as I could."

"Oh... I see."

"It seems Dr. Cthulhy was here too, so I didn't really need to come, but..." Dr. Cthulhy was sometimes asked to be present for important matches, just in case an accident happened. But this time, she was probably just a spectator. Or maybe she was there to keep an eye on Skadi, as her primary physician. There was no other explanation for why the arena staff would be unaware of Cthulhy's presence and call Glenn instead.

Just then, as if to substantiate Tisalia's conjecture, the sounds of an argument emerged from the neighboring room.

"Skadi, you get zero points. Who gave you permission to fight?"

"But it just had been so long ..."

"So what? Forget the fact that you're banned from fighting. I gave strict orders to the arena considering the state of your heart. Who lifted that ban?"

"The surgery's over, so I thought it would be fine."

"You thought it would be fine?! Ha! What do you think the phrase 'doctor's orders' even means?! You were recovering well, but now, who knows? There is no way you're ready for such an intense fight! You just do whatever you want and never listen to anyone... I know you've been sneaking snacks, too!"

"Wh-who told you that? No one knows about my midnight snacks... Have you been paying off Kunai, Cthulhy?"

"Shut up! You need to wake up and recognize that you're still recovering!"

"Stop it. I don't need a doctor who just nags me all the time. I'm going back to watch the rest of the fights."

"Idiot! You need to be examined to make sure all that moving around hasn't affected your recovery. We're going home now!"

"Nooo..."

"As your primary physician, from now on, I'm going to watch your every move. You'd better know that Kunai is on my side! We're going home now!"

"But I don't want to-o-o." Skadi dragged out every syllable.

The City Council representative was stamping her feet and having a tantrum. It was as if she had left her dignity somewhere and lost track of it. Tisalia had heard that Skadi worked harder than ever at her governmental duties after her surgery, and had, in turn, become more impulsive in her private life.

Tisalia had never dreamed she would be pulled into that impulsiveness, though.

Skadi's screams grew quieter and quieter. Cthulhy must have been dragging her away.

"Right, so that's the situation..." Dr. Glenn spoke.

"Well...I think I've gotten a glimpse into the daily struggles of a doctor."

"I'm sorry you had to hear that... Let's start the exam."

"Yes, thank you."

Kay and Lorna hurried to remove Tisalia's armor.

In normal matches, the fighters used weapons, so Tisalia wore armor to protect herself from unnecessary scratches. Centaurs were so powerful that heavy iron armor didn't hinder their movements at all. Of course, this only applied to normal matches. Skadi probably chose throwing moves as a way of going easy on Tisalia, but they had the opposite effect. Each time Tisalia hit the ground or a wall, the force of her own bodyweight and the weight of her armor worked against her. Even though she was wearing pads between the armor and her bare skin, pain was pain. Today, she'd gotten a taste of that in a very literal sense.

"Hmm..."

To be stared at in such a way—even by the man she loved—made Tisalia uncomfortable. Her bruising was centered on her torso, and most of her armor was on the top part of her body, from the waist up, where she resembled a human. Glenn examined Tisalia's body as if he were intent on licking it clean. No, that's a poor way to put it—there was nothing strange or sexual about the way this doctor examined his patient.

"There is no internal bleeding... I see. That's amazing, Tisalia. You are good at taking blows!"

"Of... Of course."

"Hmm. What's this..."

Glenn picked up Tisalia's right arm. She couldn't help but feel some excitement. Her elbow fell just below Glenn's line of vision. He took her hand and started rubbing her arm gently.

"Ouch!"

"Ahh, that's what I was afraid of. Your joint has locked. Probably from one of Marone's moves. I just saw her."

"Y-you examined Marone?"

"Yes, of course. I had some extra time."

What a workaholic.

No offense to Marone, but, for some reason, Tisalia was disappointed that she wasn't his first examination.

"Let's put a compress on it. I don't think it's serious, but it may start to hurt more later."

He stuck the compress on and patted the wrapping with his hand. He executed this treatment without hesitation.

"It looks like...everything else is fine. Do you feel pain anywhere else?"

"N-no. Not anywhere specific."

That was a lie. In truth, it wasn't just her right arm; her entire body was in pain. But this degree of soreness was a daily occurrence at the arena. It was nothing she considered severe enough to report to a doctor.

Glenn looked Tisalia closely in the eye. "Your neck?"

"Wh-what?"

"In the fight. There was just one blow that you didn't take well. Luckily, you weren't thrown directly on your head, but... Tisalia, you're not turning your head at all. Does your neck hurt?"

"You noticed that?!" If he had been watching the fight, then maybe she should have tried harder... But that wasn't the point.

Glenn didn't know anything about martial arts, but he could tell that she failed to take a blow? Right in the middle of a violent offensive and defensive battle between dragon and centaur? Still, even if he didn't know anything about fighting, when it came to monsters, he never missed injuries or illnesses. Glenn had opened his clinic while he was still young, and with his observant eye, he probably had the skills of a veteran fighter.

"Let me take a look... Ah, but I'm not tall enough."

Glenn only stood as tall as Tisalia's chest. It would be hard for him to examine her neck, even if he were to stand on his toes. Tisalia had no choice but to bend her legs and crouch down, but then...

"Here, Doctor."

"How is this?"

"Hey! Whoa!" Glenn was lifted into the air.

Kay and Lorna each took a side and lifted him in their arms. Lifting a single human man was an easy feat for a centaur. They watched to see what he would do.

"Hey, you guys!"

"You can see her neck much better from here."

"Th-that's not what I meant..." Glenn stammered.

"My Lady, don't move."

With that, Glenn was suddenly riding on Tisalia's back, placed there by Kay and Lorna. More accurately, he was sitting astride on the trunk of her body—the space between her front and back legs, which resembled a horse. The heat and weight of Glenn made Tisalia feel uneasy.

"He doesn't need to be on my back..."

"Oh, but I can certainly examine you easily from here. I'm sorry, Tisalia."

"Mmm?! Doctor, that's too..."

This wasn't good. Ethically...this was a problem.

"Ah, mmm!"

"I'm sorry, let me just take a look at your neck."

Tisalia whinnied. She shuddered as Glenn stroked the back of her neck.

Kay and Lorna, like Tisalia, wore protective equipment that resembled a horse's saddle. It was a traditional protective piece that could transform into a shield in a pinch.

However, the saddle shape was only decorative, and it wasn't actually designed for anyone to ride on. Furthermore, centaurs had high backs, so it wasn't easy for humans to sit astride. Unless, of course, they had the help of other centaurs.

"Mmm. Ah!"

"Tisalia, I'm sorry, please hold still," said Glenn.

"I-I'm trying... But you're on my back..." She was uncomfortable. Tisalia never had anyone ride on her back before.

"Oh, am I too heavy?"

"You're not heavy! You're not heavy at all!"

With their nearly upright torsos and long lower bodies, centaurs looked perfect for riding to humans, just like horses. But they resented being treated like horses. They were a proud species. It was said that in ancient times they had been ridden as slaves but used their knowledge of martial arts to fight for their freedom.

However, centaurs had one weakness.

"Mm. Ahh!"

Glenn's face was close. Tisalia could feel his breath and his fingers on her neck. She folded her arms across her chest to stay still as she endured his touch. The way centaurs were built, their hands couldn't reach their own back. She would never let someone else ride her, but this wasn't just anyone. This was the man she loved. She could easily cause a big fuss and shake him off her back—but she couldn't let Glenn get hurt. Her only choice was to let him conduct the exam from where he was perched.

"Ooooh!"

Glenn continued with the examination. He was thorough. Damage to cervical vertebra could be a matter of life and death. Tisalia endured her embarrassment and stayed still, counting the seconds until the ordeal was over.

Kay and Lorna were smiling—no, they were *smirking* as they watched their employer.

"Mmm... Oh, ooh."

Centaurs' backs were their weak points. They couldn't counterattack from there. Once someone got on them, they were stuck. For example, if Glenn had been an enemy in battle, he could have easily stabbed her in her unprotected back once he was riding her. To put it another way, centaurs only let those they trusted most onto their backs.

"Hmm. Tisalia, can you turn your head this way?"

"H-huh?"

She looked behind her, turning only her neck. Glenn's face was right next to hers. Even the battle-hardened Tisalia was powerless when it came to the man she loved, and she succumbed.

"It doesn't look like you're in pain. I don't think we need to worry about whiplash." Glenn wore the same professional expression as always. It was likely he hadn't even noticed. For a centaur to let a man around the same age as her sit on her back was like confessing that she loved and respected him more than anyone else in the world.

"Mmm!" Tisalia went weak in the knees at the thought and fought the feeling off with all her might.

Glenn continued to palpate her around the neck and shoulders until he had finished the exam, seemingly satisfied. Tisalia's sense of shame from the fact that she was being ridden was more intense than the feeling of being touched by Glenn.

Her only choice now would be to marry him.

Perhaps it was finally time to start thinking seriously about introducing him to her parents.

"Um, Tisalia..."

"Y-yes?"

"The exam is finished. It looks like your neck will be fine. Also... It's a bit too high for me to jump. Can you let me down?"

The saddle-shaped protective piece on her back didn't have stirrups. Of course he couldn't get down on his own.

"Y-yes. Just a moment..."

She bent her four legs to a more appropriate height for Glenn to dismount from. Even though she had been embarrassed, Tisalia felt somewhat sad as Glenn moved away from her.

Although she had bumps and bruises all over her body, she didn't have any broken bones or sprains. Tisalia breathed a sigh of relief at Glenn's final diagnosis. The fact that she'd gotten away with only a few bruises was proof that she had excellent defensive techniques. Considering she'd battled a dragon, she had essentially gotten away scot-free. So long as she applied compresses and soaked in the bath as necessary, she would recover quickly. At the Scythia mansion, they had medicinal bath herbs that worked well on bruises.

"That's all then. Take care of yourself."

"U-umm, Doctor?" Tisalia called after Glenn as he was about to leave. "Well, I... Actually, today was my promotion battle."

"Promotion battle? Oh, is that right? No wonder Skadi was there to watch."

Glenn had supposedly been watching as well, but he hadn't realized what the fight was for. Whether a fighter would move up or not was their own business, and it didn't really have anything to do with the spectators, so that made sense.

"And... Well, I moved up to rank two today."

"Really! Rank two? That's amazing! I heard promotion battles were tough, but... To reach rank two, you really must be a top-notch fighter. Congratulations, Tisalia!" Glenn said this with a genuine smile on his face.

He may be delicate, but Glenn was still a man. He didn't have strength or a ranking, but he could admire these qualities in others. And so...

"Yes, that's right! I worked so hard! I think a reward may be in order?"

"Absolutely! Let's celebrate! Where would be a good place to go..."

He took the words right out of her mouth, perplexing Tisalia. She knew he was incredibly busy, but to think that he would still make time for her... Her heart leaped with delight. Before she could ask if he was sure, Kay and Lorna spoke up.

"Perfect! We will arrange a celebration."

"We will set it up at a time that's convenient for you, Doctor."

"Oh, really? That would be great."

"I think the Giant Squid's Inn will be fine..."

"It will be a wonderful celebration."

The plans were already being made. Tisalia relaxed. Glenn had turned her down for marriage interviews many times. She suspected that he disliked her for some reason. But he certainly wasn't acting like he disliked her right now. She should change her approach.

Tisalia was used to attacking head-on, but that strategy didn't work on all opponents. Sometimes, even though it wasn't her specialty, she would have to switch to an attack with feints and smokescreens woven in.

Love was the same.

"Oh, about the celebration."

"Yes?"

"Um... Well, if possible, I'd like it to be just the two—"

Just the two of us.

She wanted to celebrate alone with Glenn. Perhaps it was a selfish thing to say. If she finished her sentence, would he think her self-centered? Even though she was ruthless in the arena, when it came to love, she could never make headway. Tisalia couldn't even say the words, "Just the two of us."

Just when she was trying to muster up the courage—

"Intruder!" Lorna suddenly cried out. She was facing the door to the medical office and waving her arms frantically.

The walls of the arena were made of stone. A dagger was currently protruding from it. Since even a direct hit with such a dagger wouldn't be life-threatening, it had to be just a diversion.

"L-Lorna! What has gotten into you?!"

"I'm sorry, My Lady. It looks like they ran away."

While Lorna was apologizing, Kay flew out of the room to chase after the intruder. There weren't many beings that could outrun a healthy centaur.

But Tisalia was confused. An intruder in the arena? Only authorized personnel were allowed in this area, and the security was tight. This was where the arena operations took place. How could an intruder get in? Furthermore, Tisalia hadn't sensed anyone else present.

"How could anyone possibly get past security?"

"I don't know. But when I saw them, I got sort of a bad feeling. Just slightly."

Tisalia felt a wave of admiration. Lorna's direct fighting ability was inferior to her partner Kay's. In this bout of promotions, Kay had moved up to rank three, while Lorna remained at rank four. Even though they were twins, they didn't have the same exact fighting capabilities. But, almost as compensation for that weakness, Lorna had sharpened what could only be called a sixth sense. She was especially sensitive to bloodlust and the presence of other people.

Maybe one of Dr. Glenn's procedures—a treatment that included a blindfold and restraints—had had an effect on her. Perhaps she would mature as a warrior someday soon.

"Did you see what they looked like? Did you see their face?"

"It was only a moment, and it was through the door since they were just peeking in, so I couldn't get a clear look. But..."

"But what?"

Lorna cut herself off. She was hesitant, as if she shouldn't say what she was thinking.

"It's fine. Keep going."

"Y-yes. Well, um..." Her trustworthy attendant looked extremely apologetic. "The presence of the intruder seemed... Well, it seemed very similar to your presence."

A chill seemed to fill the air.

It went without saying that even if there had been an intruder, there was no way that it could have been Tisalia.

But the ominous atmosphere lingered.

In the back of Tisalia's mind—actually, in the back of everyone's minds—a disturbing thought remained. They were all thinking the same thing, but no one dared say it.

Doppelgänger. Something that took on the form of others.

"Er."

Just when Tisalia should have been basking in her victory and promotion, things became creepy.

Kay came back and said she was unable to find a trace of the intruder. Everyone had grown quiet at the creepy thought of something unidentifiable.

"It's fine," Tisalia said to Glenn, who was looking queasy. "Even if it were a doppelgänger, if it shows up wanting trouble, I'll introduce her to my spear! Hohoho!"

Half of what she said was just tough talk, to make herself feel better. A doppelgänger was supposed to be some type of spirit, right? Would a spear even do anything to them? But Glenn looked relieved to hear Tisalia's loud laughter. She felt so happy to put someone else's mind at ease.

Especially a man she was in love with.

× ✖ ✖ ✖ ×

"To think someone is impersonating me on such a glorious day! I didn't even get the chance to ask Glenn if we could celebrate alone, just the two of us!"

They were on their way home from the arena. Tisalia clip-clopped down the main road. She was listing her complaints on the road to the mansion. Kay and Lorna giggled as they listened to Tisalia. They weren't making fun of her, of course. She had been distracted by the doppelgänger and unable to say something really important.

She wanted to celebrate over a meal alone, with Glenn.

"No... Not really. That's just an excuse," Tisalia said self-deprecatingly.

She knew the doppelgänger wasn't the issue. Even after the fuss, there had been ample opportunity to talk to Glenn, if she'd really wanted to. She just couldn't bring herself to say it because she lacked the courage. She was afraid that if she were to invite him to spend time with her alone, he would decline. She never lost her nerve in the arena, even against the Draconess. But with Glenn, she couldn't muster up enough courage. Why was it that she could never overcome her cowardice when it came to love, no matter how much she trained?

"Don't give up quite yet, My Lady." Lorna was giggling.

Peculiar...

Tisalia knew that, of all her attendants, Lorna was the one who was the fullest of mischief. She only pretended to be a proper lady. When she had that look on her face, Lorna was dangerous in more ways than one.

"B-but, now the celebration is going to be a big party at the inn, isn't it? There will be no chance for me to be alone with the doctor!"

"Don't think about it like that."

"This is your chance to cross that line in an open setting. You'll be the guest of honor!"

"Cross the line?! Just what do you have in mind, Lorna, Kay?"

"It doesn't matter who else is there."

"Don't worry, My Lady, you won't need to lift a finger."

"Y-you expect me to be that bold?"

Kay and Lorna laughed as they cantered away.

Tisalia's attendants were more enthusiastic about her interests than Tisalia was herself. At this rate, she'd be getting into something completely different than what she had hoped for. For example, they would order something from Loose Silk Sewing that barely covered her, then make her stand in front of Glenn while wearing it.

"Hey, wait up, you guys!"

Kay and Lorna were cantering at a fair speed down the main road.

Perhaps they were only teasing, but Tisalia was beside herself. When those two said they would do something, they did it. Then again, Tisalia would do anything if it would bring her and Glenn together. She was still too shy to expose her body to him. Actually, the way he'd sat on her back today was even more embarrassing, but that was different.

As she chased after Kay and Lorna, Tisalia felt a strong sense of impending crisis. She, who had achieved the amazing feat of being promoted to rank two, who was the heir of Scythia, who had brought honor to her name... She wasn't worried about the expectations her parents had for her, her future opponents, who would be even stronger, or even the doppelgängers that had the entire city talking.

She was worrying over Glenn and her runaway attendants.

✖ ✖ ✖ ✖ ✖

Several days had passed since the Draconess intruded and created such a dramatic scene.

"What did the doctor say?"

"He said he's free on the Day of the Golden Urn at the end of the month. What about the orchestra?"

"I booked them. They're free on that day as well."

"Good. Now that the date of the celebration is decided, we just need to send out invitations..."

"Wait... On the Day of the Golden Urn, won't the master and mistress be accompanying a caravan transport?"

"Hmm. Is that right? Well, perhaps Lady Tisalia will be more at ease if they don't attend anyway."

"You're terrible."

The couple—no, the girls—laughed out loud. They were the centaur ladies, Kay and Lorna.

For some reason, when they were alone, they assumed a strange dialogue. Normally, they looked exactly alike, but when their employer wasn't present, the graceful Lorna softened the commanding Kay, and they looked more like lovers, so to speak.

"Well, the lady will be satisfied so long as the doctor is there."

"That's true. Let's make sure he comes, even if that means tying him up," Kay said, without hesitation.

It wasn't a joke. She was dead serious.

In the central plaza, the two of them planned the celebration as they listened to Lulala sing. In their hands was a sheepskin they used instead of a notepad. There were many people who had to be invited. One woman in particular was an important guest.

× ✖ ✖ ✖ ×

"No problem!"

Lulala Heine was answering two questions that Kay and Lorna had asked her. She just happened to be on a break. She was a bit out of breath, but Lulala was as cheerful as always.

"Where will it be held? The Giant Squid's Inn?"

"Yes, the madam already gave us her permission."

"We would love to have you sing."

"Heh... You're making me blush!"

Even to Kay, Lulala looked like a cute little girl.

The audience gathered around the fountain was made up of both men and women. Her smile was so enchanting that it appealed to everyone, regardless of gender. Apparently, the Draconess had discovered the girl's talent herself, but Kay found it more surprising that the girl, with her beautiful voice, had never left the canals until then.

"Okay, I'll see you at the Inn at the end of the month."

"Thank you. We'll make sure there's a little something extra with your fee."

"Yay!"

Lulala splashed the water with her tail as the fountain rained down upon her. She looked like an innocent child. She was younger than Kay and Lorna, but she was also a friend of their employer, and needed to be treated with respect.

"Oh, and who will be attending?"

Kay and Lorna involuntarily looked at each other. They couldn't help but smile.

"Hey! Don't laugh at me!"

"W-we're sorry. Hehe."

"We have invited Dr. Glenn."

"What?! Oh, I mean, I don't care about Dr. Glenn, but..." Lulala looked all around, worried. She was easy to read.

As attendants, it wasn't their place to say it, but if Lulala's desires were fulfilled, it would make Tisalia cry. They couldn't overlook that. Tisalia's happiness was everything to Kay and Lorna. Wasn't it also their job to urge their employer to make sure that Lulala didn't beat her to the punch?

"That's all for now."

"We'll let you know when the rehearsal date is set."

There were other preparations to be made. They needed to prepare Tisalia's dress and accessories and decide the menu to be served at the inn. It would be rude to ask Lulala to just get up and sing on the day of the event, so they needed to arrange a rehearsal with the musicians. While they were contemplating what arrangements to move on to next, Lulala called out and stopped them.

"Oh, wait...umm, Lorna?"

"Yes?"

"You're good at baking, right?"

"Well, yes, I do what I can."

Kay figured that the girl just wanted Lorna to teach her how to bake. It was true that Lorna's baked goods were superb. Unlike Kay, who was only skilled with a sword, Lorna was also good at housekeeping tasks.

"I'm feeling a bit hungry… Do you happen to have anything to eat?"

"Something to eat? This is all I have with me right now…" Lorna took a biscuit out of her satchel. It was probably leftover from the ones she made for Tisalia.

"Can I have it?"

"Of course. Help yourself."

Lulala thanked Lorna and put the biscuit in her waterproof satchel. Then, with a splash, she submerged herself in the water. Lorna was a bit worried about the biscuit in the water, even if the satchel was waterproof.

"What's wrong, Kay?"

"It's nothing."

"Liar. Something is wrong."

Lorna leaned in closer to Kay's face. In times like these, the ever-sensitive Lorna was keen to know Kay's feelings. Kay and Lorna weren't actually related by blood, but there were moments when they knew each other even better than real twins. They had a connection deeper than siblings, deeper than lovers.

For example, right now.

"I was just thinking that Lulala didn't eat the biscuit. It seems a bit strange."

"Maybe she'll take it home to eat it."

"But she said she was hungry. Why would she wait and take it home? She could have eaten it here."

"So, maybe she was going to share with her siblings? She has a ton of little brothers and sisters."

"Wouldn't she say so if she was going to give it to her siblings? Plus, it was only one biscuit. Would she be able to split that up between all of them?"

"Then what?" Lorna stared into Kay's face.

"I don't know."

"That's it?"

"I'm not very smart. I just thought that Lulala wasn't going to eat that biscuit. That's all I know." Kay spread out her hands and threw them in the air with a sigh.

She tried not to think about things she couldn't know the answer to. It was as plain as that. For better or worse, it was Kay's policy not to dwell on things.

"Let's go, Lorna. We still have much to do."

"I know... Ugh."

Kay and Lorna continued to the plaza. So long as these two capable attendants were there, the celebration preparations would go off without a hitch. But it meant that they were too busy to dwell on their uneasy feelings about Lulala.

Who was the biscuit for?

Kay wouldn't learn the answer to that question until the celebration was over.

CASE 03:
The Scylla Who Kept Score
(or, The Day Off)

GLENN LITBEIT let out a sigh. He wondered how it had come to this.

As a doctor for monsters, Glenn had examined and treated many of them. However, he was only seventeen years old, and he was becoming keenly aware of the limits of his capabilities.

For example, just now.

The nearby nurse was giggling. Being laughed at didn't help him in the least.

Perhaps it was arrogance. He could work longer hours because he was young. He was capable. He tried remaining modest, but he had overestimated his own abilities somewhere along the line. All living things die at some point, but everyone, deep down, believed that they would never die. This was the same thing. Glenn had informed many monsters that they were ill, but he'd never anticipated falling ill himself.

"Well, you don't have a fever. Hehe. It looks like you passed out from overworking yourself." The nurse took the thermometer out from under Glenn's arm with a malicious smile on her face. She was part of the slime species, and even her smile was flabby.

"I'm not overworked. I was just a little sleep-deprived, so I was taking a nap. But then Sapphee said I was working too hard and made me admit myself to the hospital."

"But Dr. Cthulhy also diagnosed you as being overworked, right?"

"Everyone is making a big deal out of nothing."

"Well! You're supposed to be a doctor! Are you going to mock the diagnosis of another doctor?"

"Er..." Glenn didn't have a comeback for that.

The slime nurse laughed foolishly.

There was a large slime population in Lindworm. They were living beings made up entirely of a semi-transparent, gel-like substance, which they used to mimic human shapes. Glenn had known the slime nurse since his time at the academy, and, like Sapphee, she had entered before him. Her slimy personality hadn't changed.

"Right now, you are a patient. You will rest, understand?"

"Yes..."

Glenn had been taken to the Central Hospital that morning. Sapphee had determined that he'd passed out from overworking himself, and she had him admitted. Cthulhy examined him right away and came to the same conclusion as Sapphee. Her orders were for him to rest for three days—in other words, no work, only sleep.

It was true, he had been busy lately. He had been performing examination after examination without eating properly. He knew he couldn't keep it up forever...

But three days was far too long.

"Glenn, were you really working that much?"

"No, not that much. There's just been such a fuss about doppelgängers lately. There were a many people who said they felt ill after seeing a doppelgänger. But that's all."

"So, you had more patients than usual?"

"Setting aside the question of whether or not doppelgängers are real, most of the patients were simply upset because they believed that they saw one. That's not an illness, so it doesn't count as work."

This time, it was the slime nurse who sighed, loudly.

Perhaps it was because she was a shapeless monster who was only mimicking the human form, but every move she made was exaggerated. Her gel-like arm jiggled as she put on a disgusted act.

"This creates a problem for Dr. Cthulhy as well. You better stay in bed. If you get up and start examining other patients, then things won't go well for you."

"So that's why you have me in an isolated room..."

"Exactly! Direct orders of Dr. Cthulhy."

In other words, they didn't trust him.

Glenn was certain he wouldn't be able to relax here. The patients at Lindworm Central Hospital were all monsters. He was just itching to get to work helping them.

"But...for some reason, I get the feeling that the hospital is bustling."

"Oh, you noticed?"

The only person who came in and out of Glenn's private room was the slime nurse. He hadn't seen any other employees, but he could hear people rushing around outside his room. He couldn't be sure, but there seemed to be a strange air about the hospital.

"It's the perfect opportunity, so I would like to at least say hello to the senior doctors."

"No, everyone is busy."

"You're hiding something, aren't you?"

"No, nothing of the sort."

Glenn watched her, silent.

"Ah, well, I suppose I could tell you." The slime nurse oozed her way closer to him. She put her face right up close next to Glenn's so she could tell him the secret. Slimes didn't have actual eyes but formed unique eyeballs that resemble obsidian. She used these to look into Glenn's eyes. She smelled faintly of citrus.

"Actually...as you know, Skadi had heart surgery the other day."

"Yes." Not only did he know, he'd attended it as a surgeon. Even though Cthulhy was helping him, Glenn was the one who'd actually removed Skadi's heart.

"Well, the heart that was removed was being saved as a specimen...but now it's lost."

"What? Lost?"

"Yes! At some point, the preservation bottle was emptied!"

"That can't be true..." It was supposed to be an extremely important specimen for the Central Hospital.

What had happened to its storage and management? Even

when Glenn was at the academy, Cthulhy had given him thorough instructions on how to manage research materials. The employees at the Central Hospital had all been her pupils. It was hard to believe they would make such a rookie mistake.

"Well, that's what all the commotion is about in the hospital. It's a mess. To be honest, I've no time to be taking care of your overworked body! You need to sleep for three days, you got it? Don't make my job harder."

"Yes…I understand." He had been warned. No one trusted him.

× × ✖ × ×

Later, Glenn sat on his hospital bed, poring over a medical book he had brought from home. He'd been told to rest, but he wasn't sleepy. All he could do was read.

At first, no one came to his private room, but before long he started getting visitors, one after another. Most were his pupils—or he'd been their pupil—at the academy, who heard he had passed out from overwork. Some of them came just to tease him. The rest were his seniors. He had no choice but to give a half-hearted smile through conversations about his days at the academy. Glenn read his book and endured the teasing. He was waiting to talk to Cthulhy.

"Well now. You're still tired." That was Cthulhy's conclusion when she finally came to his room.

She said it as soon as she saw his face, laying into him. Glenn had rested for an entire day, and he had recovered his strength, so he couldn't have looked that tired. He felt well enough to return to the clinic and get back to work.

Cthulhy Squele was Glenn's teacher and the medical director of the Central Hospital. She was such an amazing doctor that, in the dragon surgery the other day, she'd sacrificed her own tentacle to save the patient. That tentacle had grown back by now, and she was spending her days as she always did, making rounds to check on the hospitalized patients.

"No, I feel much better. I slept all day, so I'll need to get back to the clinic soon."

"You will stay in bed for three days. Didn't Lime tell you?"

Lime was the slime nurse that was charged with caring for Glenn. She got the nickname because of the faint lime smell she emitted.

"Three days is overdoing it."

"Wrong answer. Why don't you think about why Sapphee called the Central Hospital? That's how exhausted you were."

"No, I'm a doctor, too. I know my own body."

If he had passed out from overworking, then bedrest was a sensible treatment. He would have prescribed at least three days, maybe even weeks, depending on the situation. But Glenn didn't feel exhausted. He was ready to admit to neglecting his health by not getting enough food or sleep, but one day of rest was enough. He couldn't leave Sapphee alone in the clinic for that long.

"If you're really that bored, why don't you do some brain exercises?"

"I would rather just be discharged."

"If you can answer this problem correctly, I will deem you cured and approve your discharge."

"Uh..."

Cthulhy cackled. As a doctor, she would never risk making such a bet with a patient who was truly critical. Which meant that Glenn was well enough to be discharged at any time. If that were the case, then he didn't want to bother with questions. He wished she would just let him go.

It reminded him of back when he was at the academy, and Cthulhy would test his knowledge and skills at every chance she got. Some things never changed, even now that he had opened a clinic of his own.

"I actually heard this from Skadi. She said that everyone has been talking about doppelgängers lately and told me to get to the bottom of it."

"Oh..." Just the other day, Glenn had heard a rumor about Sapphee's doppelgänger.

"Doppelgängers are nothing but an imaginary phenomenon. It's when you think you see someone you know in a place they would never be. There is no doppelgänger species among monsters."

"Yes, that's true."

"So, if that's the case, then who is causing this phenomenon? It doesn't seem like something a human could pull off easily, so perhaps it's a monster with the ability to mimic other forms?"

"And Skadi told you to find out what's really going on, because you're a monster expert?"

"Yes. She tends to pass off the cumbersome tasks to me," Dr. Cthulhy said, ignoring the fact that she was now doing the same thing to Glenn.

Glenn thought for a moment. Monsters that could freely change form *did* exist, so did that mean that one of those races was causing the doppelgänger phenomenon?

"Could it be some sort of disguise? No, that doesn't make sense."

"Right. If it was just changing a face and some features, then humans could pull it off using the same techniques as secret agents. But it's not as easy to mimic the bodies of monsters. Sometimes they appear as a lamia, sometimes a centaur. That's pretty far past the capabilities of a costume."

"So, it must be a special ability of a monster race." There were several races that had advanced transformation capabilities. "For example, illusions created by spiritual races such as ghosts or phantoms."

"I appreciate how quickly you hypothesize. Yes, it would be possible for spirits to use their illusions to make it seem as if something is there that doesn't really exist. But such conjurations are outside of our expertise as medical practitioners."

"Yes, you're right."

Glenn's specialties only included scientifically based medical treatment. He knew that other skills existed, such as sorcery, magic, and conjuration; there were also professions and research facilities that worked in those specialties. However, the objectivity and reproducibility of those skills were extremely low. The basic principal of the science that Glenn studied was, "If the process is the same, then the same results will be obtained no matter who executes that process." That wasn't the case in magic and conjuring. He had heard that Skadi dabbled in magic, but even if he and Cthulhy were to learn from her, there was no guarantee they would be able to wield it in the same way. Magic was an uncertain skill.

If the true identity of the doppelgängers involved conjuring, an expert would have to be called in to solve the problem.

"What are the other possibilities?"

"The slime species." Glenn answered his mentor's question right away. He was thinking about the nurse that had been taking care of him since the day before. "Shapeless beings, like slime, would be able to mimic other forms."

"That's right. As far as I know, the most basic species that can mimic forms are the slimes. Their bodies have a high viscosity with an undefined shape, and they mimic other races by changing form. However, their mimicry isn't perfect." It sounded like Cthulhy had already considered this possibility.

Glenn wondered how this could be considered a brain exercise. So far, he had done nothing but retrace the ideas Cthulhy had already come up with. The real test was about to begin. How close could he get to an actual doppelgänger? One wrong step and he could easily fail. Just like the tests at the academy.

"Perfect mimicry? That would mean..."

"Before that, let's look at some materials. These are witness accounts of the doppelgängers collected by the City Council. It will be faster to use these documents to simply determine whether the true form of the doppelgängers is a slime or not." Cthulhy brought out a stack of papers as she spoke.

The fact that she had prepared these in advance meant she had planned to present this question to Glenn from the start. He wasn't completely convinced, but he waited for her to continue with a straight face.

"I'll read them to you in order then."

"All right."

"Witness account number one. 'I-I saw a mermaid I knew in town, so I gathered up the courage to talk to her, but she r-ran away! I'm such a scary sight that even people I know run away after one look at me. I suck...' It's long, so I'll skip the rest. This was the testimony of an apprentice at the Kuklo Workshop."

"Doctor, your impressions are impeccable." The information was anonymous, but he could easily figure out whose testimony was whose. It was probably the timid cyclops he knew.

"I'll go on. The second account is from an alraune girl. 'I saw the City Council representative on the plantation. I thought maybe the representative had come out to check on things herself. This was a rare occurrence, so I went to greet her, but she rushed off without even giving a proper reply. When I thought about it later, it seemed like it could have been someone else entirely.'"

"This was Aluloona?"

Aluloona was influential on the council. Glenn had never met her in person, but if the sighting was on a plantation, then there was no mistake. And it seemed that, somehow, the doppelgänger could mimic the shape of a dragon.

"Yes, yes. That's enough of your inquisition. This is anonymous information." So Cthulhy said, but her impressions were spot-on, so the anonymity was pretty much pointless.

"Aluloona's plantation is outside the city, right? Doppelgängers are even showing up way out there?"

"Yes, it seems so."

"Hmm..."

"And the last one. 'I spotted my friend near the Waterways, so I invited her out for a drink, but she ran away. Normally, she loves to drink... I thought it was strange, so I followed her, but once we got into the Waterways, I lost sight of her.'"

This seemed to be a statement from an arachne that Glenn knew personally. He remained impressed with Cthulhy's voice impressions. They said some octopi could mimic sea serpents or sea anemones, so maybe that had something to do with it. The scylla species may be good at mimicry...

"Impressions, huh?"

There were three eyewitness accounts. What was strange was that they all thought they'd seen a friend. The first was probably Lulala. The second would be Skadi. In the third case, they thought they saw Sapphee. In each case, the witness believed they spotted a friend and tried to talk to them, but the friend ran away.

In each case, the doppelgänger had gone well beyond mere impressions or disguises.

"Hmm."

Perhaps it should be expressed as mimicry. Glenn remembered the incident at the arena the other day. He was sure that the form Lorna noticed was a doppelgänger. Lorna was closer to Tisalia than anyone. If she said it looked like the lady, then it must be quite detailed.

"This type of monster..."

"Have you found the answer, Glenn?"

"No. I don't know for sure yet. But I want to ask you one thing..."

"What is it?"

"If I'm able to get the correct answer to this test question, does that mean that you have already figured it out?"

"Heh..." Cthulhy adjusted her glasses as she laughed deeply.

Examiners never gave tests they don't know the answers to. At times like this, Cthulhy's eyes turned a suspicious color. You couldn't tell what she was planning. The scylla species were known as the philosophers of the deep sea, and there was no way to figure out how much they knew.

"Well, I guess you'll find out soon enough."

Glenn was silent again.

"Now, let's discuss the 'perfect mimicry' issue. I have something to do before that. You don't mind, do you?"

This was how Cthulhy replied to Glenn when he couldn't give her a clear answer. But she was still giving him hints.

Glenn thought.

Cthulhy was giving him problems to solve to buy some time while she kept him in bed. Even if the problem had been something simple, Glenn would still have been stuck in bed while he figured it out. If he wanted to be discharged, his only option was to hurry and solve the problem, giving Cthulhy an answer that would earn him full points.

"Let's take a short break then."

Was this a test or a lecture? Glenn let out a deep sigh, remembering what it was like to be a student. When he thought about it, his time at the academy had been continuous hardship. That was only natural. He was aiming to become an independent doctor for monsters and absorb all the knowledge he could from Cthulhy. After overcoming his parents' opposition and enrolling in the academy, becoming a doctor had taken over his whole existence.

He'd never dreamed that the young girl who inspired him to become a doctor—Saphentite—would be enrolled in the academy as well. But, completely absorbed in his studies, Glenn hadn't had anyone he could call a friend in school. Of course, there were times when he spoke to Sapphee or when they were involved in research together. *Come to think of it, I rarely spoke to upperclassmen...* It hadn't been Glenn's intention to avoid anyone. But, as the youngest and the most promising student, plenty of Glenn's seniors were probably jealous of him.

Glenn was just fourteen years old when he was at the academy. Cthulhy explicitly took him under her wing and made sure he received a thorough education. To Glenn, being at the academy meant accepting Cthulhy's unreasonable behavior and overcoming it in tandem with Sapphee. That was just the sort of place it was. *Maybe I should have made more friends...*

For example, the slime nurse right in front of him. He should have spoken to her. Lime was also an upperclassman to him, but Glenn knew nothing about her.

Once Cthulhy announced their break, she left the hospital room and came back with Lime.

The slime species excelled at mimicking the form of other races. While they were naturally amoeba-like beings, there were individuals who preferred taking on a human-like form, like Lime. They were known to be highly intelligent and have a high capacity for learning. They were certainly one of the stronger candidates for the identity of the doppelgängers.

"What is it? Why are you staring at me like that? Stop!"

"There just happened to be a test subject outside, so I brought her with me."

"A test subject? What are you going to do to me? I'm not getting a raise?"

"The way you neglect your duties, you have some nerve saying that. And you were the one in charge of managing that specimen… Don't you think you're lucky you're not getting a pay cut?"

"But?!" Lime screamed.

If you looked closely at her light-green tissue, you could see right through. She had the silhouette of a human, but since she didn't have any bones, both her arms and legs were curved. Slimes were a peculiar type of monster whose entire bodies were made up of an amorphous, gel-like substance. She smelled faintly of lime, which was her favorite food. She probably ate them quite often. In fact, there was a piece of lime still being digested inside her, somewhere around her neck.

She could at least digest it someplace out of sight...

Lime still didn't seem to know why she had been brought to Glenn's room.

"I wanted to give him a course on the slime race. You are our textbook."

"Agh, you're going to examine every inch of me? That's too embarrassing!"

Lime was wriggling around. That wasn't just a figure of speech—her entire body was moving dynamically, and she was getting excited.

"Right, so... Where were we?"

"We had just read the eyewitness statements. The doppelgängers mimicked people the witnesses were close to so well that all the witnesses were fooled. Then, we were contemplating if there were any monsters that could pull that off."

"That's right. And we all know that slimes are mimics."

Glenn looked at Lime again.

She looked like she had been poured into a human mold. Only her outline was a perfect human shape. But her flesh was still a semi-transparent, gel-like substance.

"As you can see, slimes can mimic an outline, but they can't transform enough to trick someone. They are only adjusting their pliable bodies."

Glenn nodded. He already understood all that. "Lime, I'm sorry, but would you please try to mimic Sapphee?"

"What? Glenn, are you into that sort of play?"

"What are you talking about?"

"I don't really know, but sure."

She wriggled and twisted and turned her entire body. For a moment, she looked like an indeterminate amoeba-like form. The nurse's uniform she had been wearing, and even the partially digested lime, drifted together inside her semi-transparent, green flesh. She didn't have any eyes or a nose or a mouth. She didn't look like something that could communicate with other beings, but this amoeba form was talking like normal.

Then...

"Transformation...complete! What do you think?"

Sapphee appeared.

No, more precisely, a slime that appeared to be an outline of Sapphee appeared. The nursing uniform she was wearing was Lime's, so she gave off a different impression than Sapphee. However, there was no question that the silhouette was Sapphee's. She had replicated the characteristic long torso of a lamia perfectly.

But...

"You wouldn't ever mistake this for Sapphee, would you?"

"Well of course not."

The slime laughed with Sapphee's face.

Her flesh was still semi-transparent slime that jiggled when touched. She had replicated something that resembled Sapphee's long hair as well, but there were no strands to speak of. Perhaps it wasn't possible to make pointy things with that type of tissue, because the ends of her hair had a roundish shape. If Glenn were to see her on the street, it would be clear that she was a transformed slime. It was as if someone had poured green gelatin into a mold of Sapphee for a jiggly treat.

"Well then, Dr. Glenn. Shall we spend some time together?"

The Lime/Sapphee tried acting flirtatious. Unfortunately, the voice was still Lime's, and she would never pass as a mimic of Sapphee. Cthulhy was far better at mimicking voices.

"As you see here, slimes can mimic the shape of other people. But not so much that you would mistake them for your friends or family. Even if slimes change their shape, they can't do anything about their semi-transparent flesh."

"Well, I can at least make vocal bands in my throat and talk."

"That's still incomplete. Your mainland common tongue sounds strange."

In their original form, slimes were unstructured beings and didn't have mouths or ears. They took in sustenance with their entire body and digested it directly in the body. They were only able to converse by reproducing the shape of vocal chords and ear drums when in human form.

"So, what conclusion can we draw from this?"

"The doppelgängers are not the work of slimes."

"So that means?"

"There is still a possibility it's a conjuring trick. But if that's not the case..." Glenn hesitated, not sure if he should say it, but he finally did. "There is a possibility that some unknown species has come to the town."

Lime let out an unrestrained scream.

The truth was that monsters were not monolithic. Each

species kept to their own kind, built villages, conducted business, lived as nomads, and sometimes even operated as mercenaries. The humans living in the human realm were ruled by the eastern aristocrats, but on the continent west of Lindworm, the monsters had no single ruling authority that they recognized. The various factions had teamed up in the most recent war to keep the humans from invading, but as soon as the war was over, those alliances disbanded.

To put it another way, it wouldn't be surprising if an unknown species was living in seclusion somewhere in the realm of monsters.

"Okay, not bad... Seventy points."

"Hmph." Glenn moaned.

He wasn't discouraged by the score Cthulhy gave him. He realized that his reasoning had holes in it. It wasn't enough to say that an unknown species was in town. Even with the meager information he had, he should have been able to extrapolate much more about the species itself. If he didn't somehow come up with the same conclusion as Cthulhy, he couldn't get a full score.

"An unknown species?! How exciting!" Lime figured she had been in the form of Sapphee for long enough and returned to her original form.

"Er..."

It wasn't a slime. It had the ability to transform, appeared everywhere in town, and showed itself in the mimicked form, but disappeared without really doing anything.

What did Cthulhy want from him? What was she telling him

to figure out? The doppelgängers' race? Their purpose? Their true form? Or…

Glenn thought some more. When was it that the doppelgängers first became a topic of talk in town? He began hearing about them last month. That's right, precisely during the period that Skadi had reached the first stage of recovery after her surgery.

Her surgery…

"Lime?"

"Yes?"

"Will you please give us a moment?"

"Oh no! Glenn, are you refusing me again?! I made myself look just like Sapphee for you!"

Her gel-like body jiggled as she protested.

"Lime, I'll start taking it out of your pay." Cthulhy's words were unforgiving.

"I was just leaving!" The slime nurse moved quickly and zipped out of the room.

It wasn't Lime's fault, but the conclusion Glenn had reached wasn't something he wanted spread to many people. Cthulhy must have sensed that and sent Lime away.

"Did you figure it out? Go ahead." She stroked Glenn's cheek with a slimy tentacle. "It's time for your score."

"I'm going to review the characteristics of a doppelgänger."

Cthulhy listened to Glenn speak with a smirk on her face.

"First, the ability to transform and mimic. According to witnesses, the likeness is so accurate that even people close to the individual being mimicked can't tell the difference. This astonishing ability is what sets it apart from the slime race, who are famous for transforming. This is what made me think that an unknown monster has found its way to Lindworm."

"Go on."

"Next, the doppelgängers are not taking any actions except for transforming. Their purpose is unclear. All the witnesses have a common claim: that they saw a doppelgänger, and when they approached, it ran away. It seems the doppelgängers are neither trying to be friendly nor cause harm to the townsfolk. At least at this point."

"Wow, you've already made it this far," Cthulhy chuckled. She always thoroughly enjoyed the progress of her pupils. That was why she tested them. It was like a hobby for her to watch them pass tests she gave them.

"They mimic, but they aren't doing anything else. That is a unique characteristic of doppelgängers. Which means I—no, we—already met this being."

"What could that be?"

"The heart."

Skadi's heart surgery had been a month ago. They'd succeeded in removing the heart-like growth. But Glenn hadn't been completely satisfied with the result. He couldn't figure out what the heart that had nested inside the dragon really was. Cardiac disease was the symptom, but what was the fake heart in the first place?

"That heart... Was it a shape-shifting monster itself?"

"Based on what evidence?"

"The heart inside Skadi looked exactly like a normal heart. But a tumor could never naturally take on the exact form of a heart. It makes more sense to consider that something with a will was mimicking her heart. That means it would be the same as the doppelgänger."

He'd begun feeling like something wasn't right partway through the surgery. That heart was too much like a heart. The illness that had been eating away at Skadi's body was the same as Skadi's heart in every way. But it existed in a place that didn't make sense—outside the rib cage. The heart that shouldn't exist had been in a place it would never be.

It was undoubtedly a doppelgänger phenomenon.

"Furthermore, I heard from Lime that the heart we removed has disappeared."

"Ahh... You heard that. That's unfortunate. It was a huge hint. I wanted you to come to that conclusion without hearing that. But that's fine. Let's just say you were lucky. Amazing, Glenn Litbeit. One hundred points." Cthulhy smiled as she praised her best pupil.

The heart they had removed from Skadi could move consciously and was causing the doppelgänger phenomenon in Lindworm. This was the conclusion that Cthulhy had reached, and it was what she wanted Glenn to figure out. She hadn't given him many hints, but he'd figured it out anyway.

"So, what are we going to do? Now that we know it's Skadi's heart, we have to do something."

"Hmm? We're not going to do anything." Cthulhy was calm.

"I'm just going to tell Skadi this hypothesis. Then I will fill out a report about losing the heart specimen and submit it to the council. They can take care of it after that. If they want me to continue working on the issue, then I'm sure Skadi will say something." Cthulhy laughed, clearly not worried about a thing.

Yes, it was true that letting the heart get away was their fault, but then, the removed heart wasn't really a heart. If it had been an unknown monster, then it would have been impossible to foresee it running away. And the doppelgänger uproar was beyond the capabilities of the hospital.

All of that was true, but Cthulhy's attitude was still confusing. She wasn't the heartless or irresponsible type. This reflected poorly on her, too, which made Glenn want to say something.

"I don't think that's the right approach, Doctor."

"Oh?" Cthulhy gave him a surprised look. Or perhaps it was an expression of being able to read him after knowing him for so long. "Are you giving me your opinion? What exactly do you find wrong with my approach?"

"Skadi is asking about the true identity of the doppelgänger, but that's not all. She wants the doppelgänger uproar to be brought under control."

"And that is the job of the City Council representative. That's not the job of doctors."

"Well...that's true. Perhaps this uproar has nothing to do with us. But the number of patient complaints of feeling ill due to seeing a doppelgänger is increasing."

Cthulhy groaned.

This was also the cause of Glenn's overworking himself. Most of the complaints were probably just in the patients' heads, or nothing but an illusion, but as the topic of the mysterious doppelgängers spread, the complaints would continue to increase as well.

"An increase in patients is definitely a problem..."

Lindworm Central Hospital was always busy. If a patient truly was ill, then they did everything in their power to treat them, but Cthulhy wanted to avoid the claims of people misled by doppelgänger rumors.

"In that case, what do you propose? Do you even have a clue as to how to get the situation under control?"

"I do."

"You what?" Cthulhy was stunned. She hadn't expected that answer.

"We have no more information as to what this doppelgänger is. I'm sure Skadi wants to apprehend it if possible, but..."

In Lindworm, only the patrol team, under direct orders of the City Council, had the authority to make arrests. If the doppelgänger was a monster, then the ordinances of the town would apply, and if it was putting the town in an uproar on purpose, then it could easily be arrested for disturbing the peace. However, Glenn didn't know what Skadi thought of the situation, and she was the one in control of the patrol team.

The bigger problem was whether the doppelgänger could even be apprehended.

"Putting the arrest aside, is Skadi interested in trying to have a conversation or even reason with it?"

"Well, first of all, we need to find out where the doppelgänger is."

"If Skadi could do that, then she wouldn't be in such a bind."

Right.

He didn't know if Skadi hadn't realized this, or if she had but wasn't ready to accept the truth. Considering the fact that the doppelgänger hadn't been found yet, it was likely the former.

"My clue is water."

"Water?"

"The witness accounts you read were all related to water. The witness who saw the mermaid and the sighting in the Waterways."

"Wait a minute. What about on the plantation?" Cthulhy had a point. "What did that have to do with...?" But her voice rose as she figured it out mid-sentence.

"The irrigation..."

"That's right. The plantation has an irrigation system for the crops. So, the doppelgänger's relationship with water—"

"No, I disagree. You don't get any points for that conjecture," Cthulhy shook her head. "Skadi collected all the witness testimony in the city. I didn't hear anything about sightings only near water, and there must have been reports from places that had nothing to do with water. If there were such a trend in the sightings, then Skadi would have noticed. So, I'm sorry, Glenn, that presumption is—"

"Doctor, I never said that there were only appearances near water."

"Huh?"

So, Skadi hadn't noticed. Glenn had been wondering: Why

did the doppelgänger appear in unexpected places at unexpected moments? Even though it was mimicking people of the town, the patrol team would have already apprehended anyone lurking suspiciously where they weren't supposed to be, even if they had to put up a net.

So why hadn't the doppelgänger been picked up?

"I think the doppelgänger is using the Waterways and rivers to move."

"How did you come to that conclusion?"

"The proof is that even with all of this sighting information, the patrol team hasn't caught it yet. There aren't many aquatic beings on the patrol team, right? When they're searching for the doppelgänger, the water is a blind spot for them. It's slipping through the cracks of their surveillance."

"Glenn, wait a second. According to that logic..."

"Yes. The doppelgänger is clearly and consciously running away from the patrol team."

Cthulhy was silent.

It wasn't just a being that was mimicking people without a purpose. The doppelgänger was staying off the patrol team's radar, only moving through the Waterways. It understood that the patrol team wasn't effectively patrolling the water.

"Actually, the other day we sighted a doppelgänger at the arena. The day that Tisalia was promoted."

"Ah, yes. The day Skadi made such a grand entrance... But you mean the doppelgänger infiltrated the arena? Isn't the security tight there?"

"Yes, it is. The only conclusion is that it timed its entrance to when the security was changing guards, or it understands which paths are blind spots. Either it is escaping the security or outsmarting them."

It was behaving like a secret agent or military operative: absolutely no wasted moves. The doppelgänger had intelligence that couldn't be underestimated. If it could evade the security at the arena, then it was possible it could also evade the Lindworm patrol team.

"It knows where the patrol team personnel are stationed, when they change shifts, and where they patrol. So, it's using the Waterways to outsmart them."

"Yes, well, there is still the question of how they attained that information. Even though Lindworm isn't a canal city, there are plenty of places in the town they can reach using the Waterways. That is why the doppelgänger appears in unexpected places at unexpected moments."

"We should probably tell Skadi."

Was this really just the work of one monster?

It knows and analyzes the movements of the patrol, who are supposedly posted all over the town. Is that even possible? It sounds impossible without a group of people, like a covert spy unit.

"At this point, there still haven't been reports of anyone being harmed by the doppelgänger... But if it's eluding the attention of the patrol team, then it would be better to secure it before something happens."

"No, Glenn, that's too passive. It has already caused harm."

"Huh?" *Was there any mention of that in the eyewitness accounts?*

"Did you forget that it was living as a parasite inside of Skadi? We might not know if it was causing harm intentionally, but it certainly got up and walked out of the hospital on its own accord. As Skadi's primary physician, I can't just let that go. And I can't let anyone become infected with the same illness as Skadi."

Glenn felt reassured.

Cthulhy wasn't irresponsible. Even after the major surgery was complete, she was concerned for Skadi's welfare. She was also deeply concerned that the doppelgänger might create more patients in the same way. Cthulhy still had her pride as a doctor. But if that were the case, then she should have said so from the beginning instead of acting indifferent. It was things like that that made people mistake her for a lazy doctor.

"Narrowing down the doppelgänger's behavior is a huge step. Skadi will be pleased."

"Well, I hope we can find it."

"If Skadi asks you to do something, make sure you help her out. Okay, Glenn?"

"I'll do my best." Glenn nodded. That was something he didn't need to be told. If this was the cause of Skadi's illness, then the issue couldn't be ignored. "That's another reason then... Doctor, I need to be discharged as soon as possible."

"Oh, right. About that, Glenn..." Cthulhy stretched out her eight tentacles toward Glenn.

Alarms went off in his head as he remembered his experiences during his time at the academy.

"Not only did you answer exactly what I was thinking, you realized the detail about the Waterways, which I hadn't even considered. You've really come a long way, Glenn. Or perhaps I'm getting old."

"N-no, we just had different perspectives."

"But Glenn. You need a break. Get some good rest."

"B-but you promised!"

"Yes, yes. I'm a liar and I don't keep my promises. I'm a bad girl," Cthulhy said coolly.

Glenn jumped out of bed and ran, trying to escape Cthulhy's evil powers. But his poor physical capabilities were no match for her expandable tentacles.

"Uh-ugh."

"If you'd like, I'll lay down with you. As the hospital director, of course."

Her tentacles, covered with a sticky substance, grabbed Glenn by the leg. Just when his feet were taken out from under him and he thought he was going to topple over, she held up his torso with another tentacle and wrapped the rest around him. This made him feel more nostalgia than pain.

He wasn't proud of it, but Glenn had a great amount experience being wrapped up like this in his line of work. For example, Sapphee's snake body, Arahnia's spider web, etc. But the reality of it was that no one had wrapped him up more than Cthulhy. Her tentacles, with the suction cups that pulled at him so hard it hurt, were familiar from his academy days.

"So, you never intended to keep your promise then?"

"That's right. The doppelgänger problem was so difficult that I hoped you would puzzle over it, and that it would keep you resting in bed. But then you answered it so quickly! That was unexpected. You get 120 points, Glenn."

So, she hadn't thought he'd be able to solve it in just one day.

Cthulhy's tentacles pulled Glenn back into bed. He tried resisting, but the more he fought back, the stronger their grip became. Scylla tentacles were solid muscle and couldn't be shaken off easily. Glenn wished Cthulhy wouldn't touch him so much. Her tentacles were making his hospital gown sticky.

"No, no, no." Cthulhy laughed at Glenn's attempts to escape, as if he were a child. "Maybe the bad little boy would like a lullaby?" She made a squishy sound as she moved her face close to Glenn's.

The expandable tentacles also carried her own body. She embraced Glenn with both arms, in addition to her tentacles, as if she were holding him in a full nelson from the front. She pushed him down onto the bed. Her tentacles were no longer holding his arms, but her entire body was now on top of him, making his scrawny arms useless.

"D-doctor... You're heavy."

"How rude."

"No—but..."

"I've focused too much on teaching you medical jargon and forgotten to teach you how to treat a lady. This is the perfect opportunity, so I'll teach you now."

Just under Cthulhy's skirt, between the tentacles, there was a web-like membrane. She placed this membrane over Glenn, as if she were covering him with a blanket or a tent. It was nice and cold. He thought he could get used to that feeling.

"You're not a boy anymore, but I still love you." She moved her face closer and whispered in his ear as if they were lovers.

"D-doctor... This isn't the way you treat patients, is it?"

She had scolded Sapphee time and again for intimacies in the clinic, and now she was doing the same thing in a hospital room while her subordinates weren't looking.

"Hmph. How rude. Even when I like one of them, I keep my hands to myself...usually..."

Glenn was getting more and more annoyed. His mentor was selfish. She did whatever she wanted without reflecting on her behavior. She'd broken her promise and pushed him down onto the bed even though she was in the middle of work. She was ordering him to recuperate while at the same time tying him up in her tentacles. He'd put up with her abuse this long only because she was his mentor.

But right then, he'd made a decision. This time, he would make her think about her behavior.

Yoink. Glenn plucked Cthulhy's glasses from her face. Luckily, both his arms were still free. But everything below his belly button was held to the bed by Cthulhy's tentacles.

"Hey! What are you doing, Glenn? Did you think you could run away if you took my glasses? I may be near-sighted, but so long as I have my tentacles, I can still find you, even with my eyes closed."

"Yes, I'm sure you can." It wasn't his intention to impair her vision. He just didn't want her glasses to get in the way of his imminent attack. "Doctor, I'm sorry."

"What?"

Glenn went for it. He touched her right on her unprotected forehead.

"Aaggghhhh! Glenn—what—you!" Cthulhy's voice echoed in the tiny room.

Glenn had never heard her use such a high-pitched tone before. If anyone saw this scene, they would surely be confused as to what was going on.

"Mmmaaaaah!"

Each time Glenn touched Cthulhy between her eyes, she trembled and gave a little jump. He was poking her gently, but her entire body shivered, as if the effect were extreme stimulation. Her tentacles trembled and stretched before going limp. Glenn's expression remained steady, as if he were using magic.

Poke, poke.

"Mmm! Ahhh!"

Poke, poke, poke, poke, poke, poke.

"Hicc! Hee! Mmm! Mmaaaah!"

Cthulhy couldn't stop trembling. Her entire body was stuck in a cycle of tensing and relaxing, and she had lost the strength to hold Glenn down any longer. He pushed her body off him, freeing himself. Cthulhy's relaxed body sprawled across the bed.

"Haaa... Hey! G-Glenn... You know what'll happen to you if you leave me like this, right?"

"Yes. You'll be scary later, so I'd better do a bit more right now."

"Hey, wait... Noo—mmmmmm!" Cthulhy let out a sound that Glenn had never heard before. She was completely powerless.

How had it turned into this? Why did Cthulhy's body keep trembling over and over, just from being poked in the forehead?

The answer was that scylla had a highly developed nervous system.

"Scylla tentacles are capable of complicated and subtle movements, as if they are separate beings. That is achieved by masses of nerves in various parts of the body. In other words, sub-brains."

"Mmmmmm! I-I know! I know that!"

"And one of those sub-brains is in the forehead."

The upper bodies of scylla were supported by a skeleton, but they didn't actually have any hard bones. All their flesh and innards were supported by cartilage. The lower half of their bodies was solid muscle. The top half looked human, but they were essentially mollusks.

To put it another way, scylla cartilage was light and durable. It protected their brains, organs, and nerves from enemies. Perhaps the cartilage was so tough because it supported their bodies in a constant battle against gravity. But the scylla forehead was relatively weak. Someone who knew as much about scylla as Glenn did could cause direct stimulation to the sub-brain under the stiff cartilage by touching the forehead.

"Oh! Ahhhh! Pleeease! Glenn, stop!" Cthulhy was screaming, with tears in her eyes.

Just from stimulation of the sub-brain, scylla could lose

control of their tentacles, experiencing intense sensations somewhere between pleasure and pain. The reason Cthulhy always wore glasses was to protect this weak point, and Glenn knew it.

Cthulhy lay on the bed, her eyes watering, drooling a little from her relaxed mouth. She was in no position to argue anymore. At this point, all eight of her tentacles were splayed out, limp.

"I'm starting to have fun, Doctor."

"Hmmm?! You scoundrel! You're actually a sadist, aren't you?! Arrrghhh!"

Glenn continued poking her forehead as he watched Cthulhy tremble. Though he didn't realize it, the trick that he was performing so casually was actually quite difficult.

"Mm! Mmm! Ah! Ahhh!"

The cartilage that protected the forehead was incredibly durable. Stimulating the sub-brain through that cartilage didn't just mean rubbing it forcefully; excessive stimulation would cause pain, resulting in a full-force reflex attack. Glenn was stimulating the sub-brain, but just enough so that the defensive instinct wouldn't kick in. It was a subtle, prescribed stimulation.

Glenn unintentionally executed this skill exquisitely.

"Mmm! Hee! Mph!"

Cthulhy's trembling tentacles began changing color, as if expressing her excitement. They transformed from a dark red to a light pink, almost white.

Scylla tentacles were like those of an octopus. When the muscles were relaxed, the tentacles were a darker color, and when flexed, the color was lighter. When the relaxing and flexing motions were repeated, the colors changed to a varying degree.

Cthulhy had her mouth closed so she wouldn't drool, but the changing colors of her tentacles revealed the truth more than her expression: this "punishment" had been effective.

Then...

"Ahhh! Ahhhhh! Mmmmmm!"

When Glenn looked up, Cthulhy's eyes were empty, and her limbs were spread out everywhere. It seemed the repeated stimulation had drained her of all her energy. Her tentacles were still trembling slightly; they didn't have any strength left to stand up. Glenn returned Cthulhy's glasses to her and completed the "punishment."

"G-Glenn... You're a technician..."

Glenn thought he may have gone too far. But, on the other hand, he also thought that this might be what it took for Cthulhy to learn her lesson. She did whatever she liked most of the time, so hopefully, she would stop abusing her authority over Glenn so much.

"Now then, I would like to be discharged."

"F-fine... It's not like I have the energy to move anyway..." Perhaps she was just a sore loser.

After thorough stimulation of the sub-brain, it would take a bit more time before she could move her tentacles. There was no one to question him returning to the clinic.

"It makes me happy that you've matured so much, Glenn..."

"Ahh, thanks."

"But…just because you outsmarted me doesn't mean you can just…do whatever you want. Don't think you'll be able to work… without running into any problems…"

Then Cthulhy suddenly fell fast asleep, as if she had used up the last of her energy. Since the director of medicine had given him her permission, the only thing left for Glenn to do was go home. Sapphee and the fairies were taking care of all his work, so he needed to hurry back and reduce their workload.

Cthulhy's breathing had turned regular, but, even asleep, she uttered one last phrase before Glenn left the room. "There's something…"

Even though it was the first time Glenn had played a trick on his mentor, all he could think about was her puzzling final words.

× ✖ ✖ ✖ ×

He walked home from the hospital.

It was already evening. That meant he'd been away from the clinic for a day and a half.

"We have been waiting for you, Doctor."

There to greet him at the door was his capable assistant, Sapphee. But for some reason, she had lifted her torso higher than usual, using the length of her lower body to tower over Glenn. Her head nearly touched the ceiling. Her expression was also sterner than usual. Her eyes were that of a snake, staring at a frog it was about to devour.

"Oh… Umm, Sapphee—"

"I heard, Doctor. You were put on bed rest, but you forced Cthulhy to discharge you. You were supposed to stay in the hospital for three days!"

"Wh—huh?"

Glenn was flustered. How did she know that? Even if she had heard from a staff member at the hospital, how could she have gotten the information so quickly when he had come straight home?

"It's a good thing I sent a fairy with you."

Sapphee opened her palm. A fairy appeared and landed directly on it. Sapphee had been so worried that she'd sent a fairy to watch over Glenn. If it were a quick fairy, it could have easily passed Glenn on the way back to the clinic.

"N-no, Sapphee. I got permission from Cthulhy to be discharged."

"Yes, yes, I know. I heard you attacked Cthulhy's forehead to get free and forced her to give you permission to be discharged. Poor form, Doctor. You shouldn't mock medicine when you're a practitioner yourself."

She knew everything.

As usual, Glenn found the face of the fairy on Sapphee's hand unreadable, but he wondered if her expression was boastful.

Sapphee sighed deeply. "But I know you had no choice but to be discharged."

"Huh?"

"As it is, Dr. Cthulhy is the director of medicine. If she gave you permission to be discharged—even if your methods were unfair and vicious—it wouldn't make sense for you to go back to the hospital now."

"Th-that's right. And there is so much work to do."

"Well then, make a choice." Sapphee had a syringe in her hand filled with medication. Her face was dead serious. "Either stay in bed and continue your treatment for one more day...or be shot full of this special anesthetic that puts even ogres to sleep. The choice is yours."

"Er... Huh?"

"You can't run away. I can easily put this anesthetic on a dart and throw it. It will knock you unconscious immediately."

If Glenn were to be shot with such a strong medication, it could put him into a permanent sleep. It was made for monsters and would be far too powerful for a meager human like Glenn.

He didn't see how he could fight Sapphee's threat.

"B-but..."

"Which will it be? Make a decision."

"Umm."

"Fine." Sapphee's eyes were stern and unforgiving.

"Ummm. Okay... Right, I'll be sleeping then."

"Good. Even doctors get sick. They get tired, too. Don't think you're special. You need to take care of yourself."

"Yes... It was my own fault."

Once he began acting cooperatively, Sapphee finally smiled.

Cthulhy probably knew this would happen. Perhaps that's why she'd let him go so easily. She knew he would be under stricter monitoring at the clinic than at the Central Hospital.

"I will take care of the work. You rest," Sapphee said. She maintained the posture of a snake lifting its head. No doubt Glenn would have to recover before she would return to her normal height and eye level.

But Glenn had an idea. He went to his room.

Glenn thought for almost an entire day as he lay in bed. He was thinking about the doppelgänger. He knew the doppelgänger was Skadi's old heart, and he also knew it was somewhere in the town and was imitating the townsfolk. The doppelgänger had a will of its own.

But what sort of will? Did it plan to nest in the body of a monster again as it had with Skadi? There hadn't been any reports like that. If such a patient appeared, the doctors would be the first to hear about it.

So...what was the final goal of a doppelgänger that did nothing but repeatedly mimic people? What was it thinking?

This was all Glenn could think about as he rested. He wasn't used to being bedridden like this, but this was what came of a doctor neglecting his own health.

CASE 04: **The Golem with Altered Flesh**

THE TOWN OF LINDWORM was surrounded by a giant wall, high enough to tower over monsters such as ogres and minotaurs. It had been erected to allow the town to serve as a fortress and withstand attempted invasions from such beings.

Inside the wall, central Lindworm was divided into districts, but the political jurisdiction of Lindworm also included the harpy village, Aluloona Plantation, and other places outside the wall. Even though it was all considered to be Lindworm, there were differences.

The gates that connected the inside and the outside were also massive. They were made to match the outer wall. Apparently, they had originally only been large enough for humans to pass through, but ever since monsters began living in Lindworm, they'd been remade so any species could pass through.

That day, Glenn Litbeit walked to the northern gate of the town.

"Oh..." He saw the hustle and bustle at the gate and sighed in admiration.

He could hear many residents at the gate, which served as the border of the city proper. There were likely merchants coming and going, gatekeepers inspecting them, and guards watching over them all. There was probably a customs officer checking goods as well.

The duties on food items in Lindworm were cheap, so many merchants brought in specialty items from the mainland. The gatekeepers and guards conducted strict inspections to make sure nothing dangerous, like weapons or poisons, was brought in.

There were also merchants on their way out. Merrow Waterways glass, cyclops-made blades, and arachne silk—all manufactured in Lindworm—were traded everywhere.

Glenn spied a group of armored centaurs, but they were probably the caravan, the pride of Scythia Transportation. They didn't just transport goods, but also protected the cargo from brigands and bandits, and were thus deemed extremely reliable. Glenn figured that from here, they would cross over the mountains, transporting their cargo to distant lands.

There were also a few who looked like travelers and tourists. The north and west gates led to a mountain road that connected to the monster realm. Monsters could use this road to travel to Lindworm without the hardships of crossing the mountain. Between the arena and canal, tourism was also an important industry in Lindworm.

"Dr. Glenn."

As he was staring at the checkpoint, he heard a voice call out to him. It was the person he was there to meet.

"I'm sorry to have made you wait. We've had our hands full lately."

"Not at all. I've only just arrived myself."

"Oh, really? That's all right then."

It was Kunai Zenow.

Kunai was a flesh golem, made by stitching corpses together. She was the bodyguard of the City Council representative, Skadi, but it seemed that, with her newfound vitality, Skadi had been ordering her around more than usual lately. Maybe that was why her face looked so pale. No—her face always looked like that. And her right arm was cut clean off, just like Glenn had heard.

"I heard you were in the hospital for being overworked. Are you okay now?" she asked.

"It really wasn't a big deal in the first place. Sapphee finally gave me permission to be up and about, so it's fine now."

"Sapphee, huh?" Kunai narrowed her eyes. "Did Sapphee say anything to you when you told her you were coming to the north gate today?"

"Yes, she did... She asked if I was leaving her behind to go on a date with Miss Kunai. She asked where we would be going."

"And what was your answer?"

"I just told her where we are going. Then she shut up right away."

"That makes sense." Kunai chuckled as they went through the gate. Normally, going through the gate required an inspection, but someone with the status of Kunai was able to go through without being bothered. "Who would ever go to a graveyard city on a date?"

× ✖ ✖ ✖ ×

The official name was Deadlich Graveyard City.

It was often simply called "graveyard city" or "the graveyard district," and it was located just a little ways from the north gate of town.

To put it simply, it was a mass grave created on the outskirts of the city.

Part of the Vivre River, which flowed down from the mountains, also flowed into the Waterways. The main stream passed through the north side of Lindworm then curved over to the west side of town. The graveyard district was just on the other side of the arch-shaped stone bridge that crossed over the Vivre River.

No human or monster could escape death. There were graves lined up over the hilly area, and many people from Lindworm were buried there. This was the final resting place of townsfolk who had passed away.

But this graveyard in the suburbs also served another function.

"I heard that there are incorporeal monsters, like wraiths and ghosts, and undead monsters, like zombies, skeletons, and liches, living here..."

"Yes, well, perhaps it is a place you wouldn't normally have reason to visit."

"Yeah, I guess a doctor's job ends once the diagnosis is death." Glenn had examined many patients. And in cases where every means had failed, he'd had to write out death certificates. But after a patient's death, they were the ward of the undertaker.

"One of the major problems the Draconess faced when she was trying to build a town where humans and monsters could cohabitate was how to handle the undead. She didn't want to discriminate, but it was easy to imagine certain issues that could arise if they lived in town. For example, the elderly complain that the smells of decay and death are bad omens. Another example is that ghosts tend to haunt residents if they have free time on their hands..."

"Well, when you put it like that, it sounds like nothing *but* problems."

The outskirts of Lindworm were just as divided as the inside. Outside the wall, there was the harpy village on the mountain, the Aluloona Plantation that spread over the plains, and the Deadlich Graveyard City located in the hills.

"There are some undead living in town of course."

"Ahh, yes. There is a zombie named Frank who lives near the clinic." Glenn recalled a patient of his who came in periodically to pick up preservatives. Frank was a quiet gentleman.

"However, those are the exceptions," Kunai continued. "They need to groom and take measures against odor, and, even if they do, it's hard to describe the way the dead are viewed. Even in Lindworm."

"They're categorized not in terms of humans and monsters, but in terms of the living and the dead..."

Even Frank, who lived in the town, was a bit of an oddball.

The road that led to the graveyard city was on a slight incline. After a few minutes, they could see a graveyard surrounded by a fence. But this was only a normal cemetery. The residents of Lindworm came here to visit the graves of the deceased. This was the public facade of the district.

The graveyard city that served as living quarters was behind that, in the ruins.

"So, the Draconess turned the unused ruins into a district where the undead could reside—that is, she turned it into the graveyard city. They say it used to be a small village, but no one was living there anymore because of the war. I rent an apartment there, though I rarely use it. I'm usually on night watch for the City Council."

"Oh, I see."

Kunai was also one of the undead. There was nothing strange about her renting a home in the graveyard city.

"It's also easy to see why there is a river between the town and the graveyard."

"What do you mean?"

"They say that the dead and vampires can't cross over running water. Of course, it's only a superstition, but, symbolically, a river is probably the perfect border between the living and dead."

So, a clear line has been drawn by placing a bridge between them.

At that point, they were just crossing over the stone bridge. Aquatic monsters were fishing and harvesting waterweed. The

Vivre River was an important water source for Lindworm, which was located inland.

"Like me, the people who live in Deadlich generally come here to live on their own accord. They figure it's not good for a city to have too many undead. There are also those who find it more comfortable to be surrounded by beings like themselves."

The undead. Or, the already dead.

There must be extraordinary hardships that came with such an existence. Glenn felt like he could understand the sentiment of the undead who chose to live on the outskirts of town.

They finished crossing the bridge and continued up the hill. At last, they could see a steel fence and a rotting gate. The area surrounding the gate was overgrown with ivy. A small lizard skittered around as if to greet the guests. It was dark, even though it was the middle of the day. The sky had been clear back in Lindworm, but now it was overcast. Glenn wondered if it was normal for the weather to change so quickly here.

"The darkness is from the miasma. Don't worry about it."

"That's easy for you to say..."

"I'm currently serving as the acting manager for the graveyard city. Nothing will happen to you."

Creeeeak.

The sound the gate made when Kunai opened it was exactly like the scream of a living being. It was as if the rusted gate was a mouth opening.

"Welcome to Deadlich Graveyard City, the town that doesn't need doctors." Kunai spoke as if she were reciting the lines to a play. After she said it, she let out a small cough, like she was embarrassed. "Sorry… My chin and neck are from a deceased theatrical actor. But it doesn't suit me."

"Not at all. You were very good."

"No need for flattery." Kunai turned away.

They entered the gate, and Glenn saw a town made of ruins. In front of the small square were rotting homes and apartments. There was a stand that seemed to sell food, but its outer walls were peeling, and it didn't look like it was open.

"The big building in front is called Deadlich Hotel. That's the only facility that serves tourists, so it's clean inside. It's the only place in the graveyard city that outsiders are allowed in."

"Do tourists actually come here?"

"Sometimes. They come to test their courage."

Glenn was dumbfounded. It certainly wasn't the Waterways, but it *was* a tourist attraction.

Putting his thoughts aside, Glenn surveyed his surroundings.

There was a zombie with a half-rotted body leaving the ruins. He greeted Glenn when their eyes met. His perfectly preserved eyes looked straight into Glenn's, and it was clear that, even though he was dead, his consciousness was completely intact.

Glenn felt others watching him from the direction of the hotel. When he glanced in that direction, he saw a pair of shining eyes. They were the eyes of a nocturnal animal.

"Don't stare too much. There has been a family of vampires staying there for about six months."

"V-vampires?!"

"They're not the sort to randomly attack people, but they do take notice of fresh blood." She said this so nonchalantly.

Glenn grew pale. He had heard the people here—well, the undead—lived as they pleased.

"I don't have any spiritual senses, so I wouldn't be able to tell, but are there dead spirit monsters like ghosts and wraiths here too?"

"Of course. There's one in there." Kunai pointed behind Glenn's back.

"Er..." Glenn turned around, but no one was there.

He didn't understand magic, but he trusted Kunai when she said it was there.

It was said that both humans and monsters became ghosts if they died still holding a grudge. In other words, the spirit would escape and go out on its own.

"I can understand that corpses and bones can move because of magic or mystical forces...like you, Miss Kunai. But the incorporeal monsters... I've read about them...though I've never seen one..."

"That's their nature. They don't go out of their way to get close to those who can't see them, even people they know. Warding off ghosts is the job of priests. Oh, but you should carry this." Kunai handed him something with her left hand.

It was a small amulet embedded with a jewel. It looked like it was meant to be worn as a pendant around the neck, but there was no string or chain. Glenn had no choice but to put it in the pocket of his white coat.

"It's a safeguard made by the Draconess. It should put your mind at ease. Be careful not to get possessed by any ghosts."

"So, this is a dangerous place..."

"Well, it was kept in better order when there was a manager, but now... Well, maybe I should tell you the whole story. Here we are. This is the church."

They had reached their destination. It was one of many churches Glenn had seen, even in the spooky graveyard city. Moss grew on the stone walls, making it feel ancient, but there were flowers growing in the vase at the entrance, proof that someone had been taking good care of it recently.

Stranger still was the large casket in front of the church door. Of course, it was a graveyard city, so perhaps a coffin wasn't such a strange sight after all. The casket was brand new.

A new coffin was a bad sign. It meant that someone had died.

"As you can see," Kunai said, "Deadlich is a disorderly place. When the Draconess made the decision to create a graveyard city, her initial fear was that it would run rampant with beings that threatened the living. Even if it's on the outskirts, this is still part of Lindworm. We can't overlook the fact that it's getting more dangerous."

"Y-yes."

"That's why she left a skeleton in charge. Its role was to maintain order and manage the district as a citizen of the town, even if it couldn't live in the town. But the other day, the spirit of this skeleton ascended to the heavens. Only its bones are left in that coffin."

Its spirit... A shapeless concept, but still a sign of life. Were the heart and consciousness also harbored in the spirit?

Glenn didn't know the answer. To him, as a doctor, life was dependent on the functioning of the body's organs, starting with the heart and the brain. The flesh of living beings operated through a series of continuous cycles, and living things metabolized, proof of their health.

A person didn't need a soul to live. When he performed autopsies, there was no soul. And the residents of the graveyard city were living, even if they didn't have any. Or, perhaps they were living *only* on their souls. He felt like he was about to fall down the philosophical pit of the meaning of life itself.

"The manager...died?"

"You could also call it 'nirvana.' The spirit that was moving the skeleton lost its earthly attachments and disappeared. The only things left now are the bones."

Kunai opened the coffin. Inside was a white skeleton lying faceup with its hands folded neatly across its chest. There was a large shovel beside it; it must have been a possession of the deceased.

"Now, I have stepped in as temporary manager, but it's not going as well as before." Kunai shrugged.

Glenn didn't know what the job of the manager entailed, but he did know it probably wasn't a job Kunai would be good at.

"Honestly, the ghosts and wraiths ignore my orders and behave however they want. And I can't be here all the time... At least the zombies and skeletons listen to me, but..."

"Th-that must be a problem then."

"Yeah, it's a big problem. If the atmosphere gets too uncomfortable, the residents will have no problem breaking down the spell barrier. If ghosts get into downtown Lindworm, they'll cause a huge commotion. I've increased security, but..." Kunai put her head in her hands. "I don't know how the skeleton kept them in order. The only way I know to get people to listen is to hit or kick them... What can I do?"

"What did Skadi say?"

"She said she'll find a successor as soon as she can. She told me to 'hang in there.'" Kunai's face was somber.

Since the orders were from Skadi, she couldn't just abandon the job, but...there *was* such a thing as job compatibility. Or lack thereof. Kunai's only specialty was combat, and she probably had no business doing administrative work.

"D-don't give up."

"Yeah." Her reply was emotionless. But it wasn't as if a mere doctor like Glenn could get involved in politics. All he could do was offer words of encouragement.

"But...I'm confused by the title. Why 'manager'? I would understand something like 'administrator' or 'mayor'..."

"It was originally meant to be the manager of Deadlich Hotel, in the center of the graveyard city. My predecessor was great at dealing with customers and tourists, and the hotel was also highly rated. I'm really not much of a replacement."

"Oh."

It seemed the graveyard city had its own problems.

"Enough talking. Let's do what we came here for."

"Oh, yes."

The unique sights of the graveyard city had been burned into Glenn's retinas, and he had almost forgotten why he'd even ended up in this graveyard city—Kunai's severed arm. It was time for him to get to work.

Kunai closed the lid of the casket that held the previous manager and turned to the back of the church. Glenn followed her.

"Ohh!" Glenn cried out at what he saw.

"This is the dead flesh I collected for today. What do you think? Not bad, right?" Kunai seemed proud of herself.

In the backyard of the church was a pile of dead flesh. A mountain of right arms, indiscriminate of age or gender, towered over them.

"Does it make you feel ill?"

"N-no..." This was the reason he had come.

Kunai Zenow had buried the right arm she'd been using up to that point in the ground. According to her, even dead flesh harbored something like a soul. After gently burying whichever part of her she had previously used, she searched for dead flesh to replace it on her body.

Glenn's job today was to procure and attach Kunai's new right arm.

"There are so many..."

"I'm not the only one. Many undead use corpses. The old manager stored the unburied corpses in the church and supplied them to the undead when necessary, as well as to me. Many times..." Kunai trailed off.

"Is that so? Wow! This arm has been preserved perfectly."

"The manager was trained in embalming."

Even just a glance at the arm made it clear to Glenn that the previous manager had been extremely skilled. Lindworm was already a cool and dry climate, where corpses often turned to wax without rotting. If, on top of that, someone trained in burial techniques were to take appropriate measures, it would be possible to preserve a body for years...or even decades.

"Most of these arms were collected from the bodies of human and monster warriors during the great war."

"Does that mean no one dug graves or mourned for them?" Glenn asked.

"Yeah, or some had injuries so severe that the body couldn't even be identified."

After the war, there had probably been few bodies in a recognizable state. They were those cut by blades, crushed by blunt weapons, shot with arrows... There were probably burned corpses as well, and those eroded by epidemics. There would have been very few left all in one piece.

Kunai went on. "Part of the manager's job was to store those corpses and occasionally provide them to the residents. My predecessor also thought of it as a sort of memorial to those who died in war."

"I see..." It seemed clear that the previous manager had possessed a great respect for life and a deep knowledge of undead monsters. Glenn regretted that he hadn't been able to meet the skeleton before its passing.

"Dr. Glenn, once we find a good arm, I need you to sew it on for me."

"Yes." Glenn nodded.

He was genuinely happy that Kunai, who had hated doctors at first, now trusted him so much that she'd selected him by name for her medical needs.

"Well then, let's pick out an arm."

"Dr. Glenn! Dr. Glenn!"

Glenn was resting on the stone steps in front of the church when he heard Kunai's voice calling him.

"How about this arm? It belonged to an ogre soldier who attacked Lindworm! Imagine how well I could protect the Draconess with an arm like this!"

He looked at what Kunai was holding.

It was a massive arm that looked to be as long as Kunai was tall. Of course, it wasn't as large as the Giant Goddess Dione's arm, but it must have belonged to a huge monster. There were also several small scratches on the arm, the marks of a seasoned soldier. It was stout and muscular, unmistakably the arm of a male ogre.

"Sorry, it's a bit..." Glenn didn't know where to begin.

"What? Is it weird?"

"It's too heavy. Even if I were to sew it on, the thread wouldn't be able to hold it, and the stitches would shred your skin."

"Humph… I thought it would be good."

Glenn continued. "Even if we were to attach it with wire instead, the balance would be a problem. Your center of gravity would be lopsided. You'd have a hard time standing up."

"Well, that would be pointless. I get it. I'll look for a smaller arm."

Kunai only seemed concerned with whether the arm would be good in a fight. What about her everyday life? If Glenn hadn't been there to step in, Kunai would have combined all the strongest monster parts she could find. Glenn could just see it: She'd have the right arm of a giant, the left arm of a beast, the lower body of a centaur, the scales of a reptile, the wings of a harpy, and so on.

He tried imagining what Kunai's final form might have looked like. She would have been too conspicuous to serve as Skadi's bodyguard, and the mismatched body would have also likely gotten in the way of her daily activities.

Yes, if he didn't step in, Kunai would only look for outlandish limbs. Part of Glenn's job was to put the brakes on her.

"Dr. Glenn! How about this one?" Kunai was already bringing him another arm. It must have been exciting for her to attach new flesh to her body.

"Ahh, a human arm. That would be better."

"Right? And look at the elbow."

Shiiing.

The arm made a metallic sound that never could have come from dead flesh alone. The elbow bent in a way unnatural for a human joint, and something resembling a sword blade jutted out.

A sword blade?

"Is that a hidden sword?!"

"Yeah. I heard that during the war there was an army of humans who altered their bodies. Maybe this belonged to one of them! This is amazing technology. If the workshop could maintain it, it would be incredibly practical."

"That story..." Glenn was about to say that he'd never heard of such a thing, but then he stopped himself. He remembered that Kunai Zenow had been created for the purpose of raising an undead army. If someone was researching that, then meddling with human alterations couldn't be so hard to believe.

Compared to creating life from dead skin, it would be much simpler to embed weapons in living skin...wouldn't it?

"It's downright sinful. But it would be useful for me." Kunai looked like she was enjoying herself.

Someone as skilled at fighting as Kunai would be able to use this hidden-sword arm to its full potential. But there was a problem.

"Hmmm..."

"It won't work?"

"I'm worried about the weight," Glenn said as he took the arm from her. Even though it wasn't as heavy as an ogre arm, the hidden metal still weighed the arm down. "If you really want to use it, it would be better to install metal into the rest of your body as well... but to do that, I think you'd need to ask a workshop, not a doctor."

"Ugh. I don't really want to mess with my body."

"Yeah."

"I've also already ordered exoskeleton armor from the workshop. I'm going to ride in it so I can be more effective than even the giants. I can't order anything else."

"What do you mean...?"

"I have the blueprints. Wanna see?"

Why is she carrying something like that around?

The sheepskin Kunai pulled out had blueprints for exoskeleton armor. They were hand-drawn, but as far as Glenn could tell, the exoskeleton was a massive steel suit that wrapped around the wearer. The overall size rivaled that of a giant.

"Does this...move?"

"They said it's steam-powered. The person riding in it feels like they're in a steam bath because of the exhaust, but that's not a problem for me."

"I would guess not."

"But they said it will take ten years to complete."

"I wish you would come up with a more realistic armament."

Kunai was clearly very serious about this, but the cyclops who had to make it were probably beside themselves. Glenn wished he could have seen the look on Memé and the boss's faces when they saw these blueprints.

"I'm sorry, I know that fighting ability is important to you, but...please choose an arm that will take care of you, too. If the size and weight aren't suitable to your body, I won't even be able to attach it in the first place."

"Humph. Just when I found an arm over there with a gun in the pinky finger."

"No, Miss Kunai. Think about it. This will become a part of you. There has to be something like what you had before...a perfect fit."

"Humph. Humph. Humph..." Kunai groaned for a while. She held her head in her hands and shook it from side to side. Except when Kunai did that, it looked like her head would pop off and roll away.

Finally, she approached the mountain of flesh again and started hemming and hawing over the arms. It seemed like she was only selecting human arms, or arms that resembled a human's. But when Glenn came closer, he could tell she was muttering something. He pricked up his ears.

"You...humph. So, you *did* die in a war. What, you don't want to be part of a woman's body? I don't think you're in a position to complain. How about you over there? You want to go back to your old body? Fine, then stay there. How about the young one over there? Mmm hmm. I see, you want to go back to your home..."

She was having a conversation.

While Glenn was sure it was impossible to converse with dead flesh, it was hard to deny when he could see Kunai talking to it with his own eyes. But he couldn't hear the voices of the dead flesh. He wondered what made Kunai so different that she could understand the consciousness of the parts.

Everything Glenn had seen since arriving in Deadlich Graveyard City today had surprised him. Corpses could move, spirits were roaming about, and right in front of him someone was having a conversation with dead flesh. And that someone was a corpse herself. The place was overflowing with death. But it wasn't as if the living were banned from this place. The graveyard city actually existed, and it wasn't heaven or the underworld. This was also part of Lindworm, which meant there was work for him here.

But...

He got the feeling that he shouldn't be listening to Kunai's conversations with the dead flesh. This was a private issue between her and whichever limb would soon become a part of her. That was why she was mumbling in such a low voice.

Glenn moved away from Kunai. A spot of light was burning in front of the church. It was a will o' the wisp, standing out against the dark ambiance of the graveyard city.

"Eh."

Will o' the wisps were made by ghosts. Glenn couldn't see spirits with his own eyes, but he could see the phenomena they made, such as this light. He felt uneasy. The will o' the wisp flickered closer.

"This..."

I have to run away.

That was what he was thinking, but he couldn't move. He was locked in. The ghost who'd made that will o' the wisp clearly had its eyes on Glenn. Side effects of being possessed by a ghost included chills, nausea, headaches, hallucinations, etc. The victim would then lose consciousness, and the ghost would steal their life force.

Damnit. I shouldn't have moved so far away from Kunai, Glenn thought.

Thinking was all he could do. The wisp had frozen him in his tracks.

"...?"

What?

The wisp had stopped moving, as if it were afraid of something. Glenn remembered Skadi's amulet in his pocket and pulled it out.

"I'm very sorry... I don't have time to be possessed."

When he held up the amulet, it seemed to have an immediate effect on the will o' the wisp. It rushed away and disappeared into the dark, deep in the heart of the graveyard city. It seemed the Draconess' powers weren't to be trifled with.

"It looks like this place really isn't safe."

It was clear now why they'd gone out of the way to put this place on the outskirts of town. The fact that he'd never heard of any problems in the graveyard city reflected the previous manager's competence. It must have been amazing.

"Dr. Glenn, did something happen?" He heard Kunai's voice from the backyard.

"No, I'm fine." Even though Glenn had been able to ward off that ghost, he decided to return to Kunai's side, just in case.

Behind the church, Kunai had finally found a good arm. She looked pleased with herself.

× × ✖ × ×

"What do you think?" Glenn asked, after he had finished sewing on the arm.

After repeated conversations with the dead flesh, Kunai had finally found a suitable right arm. It was a bit skinnier than the arm she'd been using before, but it was toned and muscular. It was probably the arm of a soldier who had died in battle. It didn't have the obvious sort of fighting strength that the ogre arm had, but the slender arm seemed like it would mesh well with Kunai's body.

After preparing the opening of the right arm with his surgical knife, Glenn sewed it on with a needle and thread. He was able to attach it as if it had always been part of her. But there was one thing Glenn didn't know: the dead flesh parts had already accepted that they would be connected to each other. The result was that Glenn, who had sewed parts onto Kunai countless times, stitched her new arm on so well that it looked like she had been born with it.

"Hmm?"

"I actually think I did a fair job on the stitching, but..."

"You're right... For a new arm, it already gives me such a sense of unity... It's almost scary. Thank you, Dr. Glenn." Though she was praising him, her expression was a bit too somber. She repeatedly open and closed her fist, punching the air. "But... Oooh. Something is weird."

"What do you mean, 'something'?"

"It's light. The arm is too light." Kunai punched the air as she stepped nimbly and did a roundabout kick.

To Glenn, the martial arts exercises looked beautiful, but Kunai was cocking her head to the side, still not convinced.

"Ugh! Why can't I find my balance?!" Kunai was grinding her teeth, repeating her moves over and over, trying to get used to her right arm.

The sewing job was perfect. Even with her violent movements, the arm was functioning without any problems. By all accounts, the arm had already become part of Kunai. But Glenn worried about her calling it 'light.' The new arm was skinnier than what she'd had before, but it was a man's arm. It was a bit less muscular, but it didn't seem like there was a significant difference in weight.

"Are you talking about your center of gravity? Miss Kunai, can you try standing up with your back straight? Yes, like that... Now, stretch both of your arms straight down by your thighs. There, perfect."

Kunai followed Glenn's instructions and stood at attention. As a guard, her posture was beautiful. But Glenn immediately noticed where the discomfort was coming from.

She was tilting.

"You're crooked."

"Huh?"

"Your spine is tilted just a tad to the left. The bone is crooked, so it's making you feel off balance."

"N-no way! It was never like that before."

"You're right. There didn't seem to be any problems...before."

A crooked back.

It was something that occurred in both humans and monsters. If you kept the same posture for long hours or did forced exercises, the muscles grew stiff and the bones became crooked.

I should have noticed it earlier.

Kunai was a corpse. All her muscles were treated with preservatives and exhibited rigor mortis. In other words, they lacked strength and flexibility. Kunai's flesh was supported by nothing but bones and magical powers. Furthermore, she stood at attention as a guard sometimes, and fought at other times. He couldn't imagine how much stress she was putting on her bones.

The result was her crooked spine.

"Your old right arm was big and heavy, so your backbone subconsciously tilted to the left to balance you out. If you were human, a crooked back would make your muscles sore, and you would feel pain. But since you don't have a sense of pain, you wouldn't have noticed," Glenn explained.

"Humph..."

"Of course, it's because you're a flesh golem that you haven't had any problems so far, but..."

In humans, a crooked spine affected various parts of the body: the cervical spine, lumbar spine, and, in severe cases, subjective symptoms occurred in the shoulders and lower extremities. Of course, this wasn't limited to humans. It applied to monsters with vertebrae as well, and it could be prevented with appropriate exercise and stretching, but...

What about for a flesh golem made of corpses? The muscles are in rigor mortis, so, clearly, there is no point in stretching. On the other hand, the crooked spine doesn't cause any pain, so that's a relief.

The only problem it was causing for Kunai was the instability of her center of gravity.

"So, you mean that, since my new arm is lighter, I'm not able to balance the way I used to, and my center of balance moved to the left? That's why I feel strange?"

"Yes, that's right."

"I've become weak... How can I serve as a guard..." Kunai trailed off, perplexed, as she continued punching the air with her fist.

From Glenn's perspective, she looked the same as always, as if she could turn bandits upside down in a second. But Kunai felt a sense of dissatisfaction that no one else could understand.

"It will be okay, Miss Kunai. I can treat you."

"What? Really?"

"Of course. There is a way to treat it."

He wasn't sure that, with Kunai's rigor mortis muscles, there was any way the spine would heal naturally. But if they just left it, there was a high possibility that it would become even more crooked.

"What is the treatment?"

Glenn looked Kunai in the eyes. "Chiropractic, of course."

Glenn took Kunai inside the church.

The outside had been fairly well taken care of, but the inside was immaculate. Even the pews had been cleaned spotless. In every way, it looked like a church that was currently in use.

"The manager was living here in the church. That's why it looks like this."

"Oh."

"Well then, should I lie on my stomach?"

"Yes, please. I'll get started."

Kunai lay down on a prayer bench. Glenn covered her with a clean cotton cloth that he had prepared ahead of time. In this position, he couldn't see her face.

"It seems like that position would be uncomfortable, so...here." Glenn handed Kunai a cushion he'd found in the room.

"Ah. Mmm." Kunai held it and relaxed her entire body. Her upper body curved slightly.

When Glenn looked closer, he could see that her body was tense, as he had expected. Kunai Zenow was made up of many different parts that had come together as one—a true work of art. He didn't want to empathize with the doctor who'd made Kunai, but, in all honesty, he had to admire the skill that went into turning her body into this form.

"It would be better to do this on a bed, but let's see what we can do."

"You don't need to talk. Just get on with it."

"Right then. I'll start." Glenn put his hands on Kunai's back. The dead flesh of Kunai's body maintained the chill of a corpse.

He began by rubbing the muscles on each side of the vertebrae. When he touched them directly, the shape of the muscles and the crooked bones were clear. Kunai's backbone curved to the left.

"Mmm..."

"How is it?"

"It's curved, like I thought. It's a...pretty stubborn curve..." It wouldn't be easy to straighten out the bones with this treatment alone.

Normally, he would spend a lot of time massaging the muscles, doing repeated stretches, and slowly straightening them out. But it was different with flesh golems.

The only thing Kunai felt was a strange change in her center of gravity. Even if her bones were crooked, the pain of pinched nerves wasn't a problem for flesh golems. Their bodies were moving by magical force, so even a broken bone wouldn't be painful.

So that means...

"Kunai, do you mind if I massage you hard?"

"Hmm? Oh, that's fine."

"Okay then."

"Mmmmm?!"

Glenn slowly straddled Kunai in a position that made it look like he was riding on her gluteal region. Kunai opened her eyes wide and looked at Glenn, flustered.

"Wh-why are you on top of me?"

"This is the best position to make sure I have leverage for a stronger massage. I'm very sorry. Am I too heavy?"

"N-no, you're not heavy..." Kunai sounded confused, but she didn't refuse him.

Glenn began rubbing the muscles on both sides of her spine. Before long, he was applying enough force to move the bone back to its correct form.

"Mmm." Kunai let out a moan.

Glenn ignored it and continued. He wasn't very strong, but, as a doctor, he understood where to apply his strength—and just how much he needed to be effective.

"I'm going to go a bit harder."

"Mmm—argh?!" Kunai's voice was shrill. It was uncharacteristic of her. She always had a stern look on her face.

"Oh! Did that hurt?!"

"No-no... It's a strange feeling...but not pain." Kunai's voice had even surprised herself. "I'm not sure. It was like your finger was going inside me..."

"It sounds like it's working. I'll continue."

"No, wait a—aaaaghh." Kunai's bones cracked.

Since her muscles were stiff, Glenn thought that her bones might not move, either—but it seemed like his chiropractic skills were quite effective. Glenn continued rubbing the muscles from around the shoulder blade to the spine and used his weight to set the bone at just the right moment.

Crackle, crackle.

"Heeeee?!" Kunai's body quivered, and she screamed.

"How are you doing?" Glenn asked.

"I-I... How am I doing? M-my voice! Dr. Glenn, what type of martial arts is this?!"

"This is just chiropractic."

"N-n-no way... Th-this is... Mphaaaaa!"

Crackle, crackle, crackle.

"Arrghhh!"

He hadn't thought it would be this effective.

Glenn could tell by the sensation in the palm of his hand that the bone was moving, and better than he'd expected. In fact, the bone was moving so well that it was hard to believe the muscles were in rigor mortis. It slowly moved back into the correct position, almost as if he were touching the bone directly.

"D-Dr. Glenn... Didn't you say you don't have any understanding of magic?"

"Hmm? Ahh, yes, of course."

"Ughh! B-but maybe you're interfering with the magic supporting my body..." Kunai started to explain through her labored breaths.

"Wh-why is that?"

"Mmm! How should I know?! It feels weird, like you're touching the deepest places in my body!"

"Hmmm..."

Massages had relaxing effects. They tapped into the vitality that all living beings possessed. Hot springs, acupuncture, and moxibustion also had similar effects. The idea of assisting vitality was a medical treatment mainly developed in the east, and Glenn wasn't an expert, but...

"Vitality..."

Kunai's body was already dead. However, her body had a will and was active. That was due to magic...but perhaps it was actually a form of life.

"That might be your own power, Miss Kunai."

"What?"

"Your vitality is being stimulated by the massage. Your own

will to live is affecting the magic, and that may be what is moving your bone back to the correct position..."

"M-me? Myself?!"

Kunai's curved bone was being fixed, triggered by Glenn's chiropractic treatment. If it wasn't Glenn's strength—if that was merely the catalyst for Kunai's own bones to move themselves back to the right position—well, that would be an interesting phenomenon indeed.

"W-wait. If that's true, then what is this numbness..."

"I think perhaps it's the effect of interfering with the magical field of the spell..." It wasn't his intention, but Glenn was affecting Kunai's core magic. It was only natural that she would also feel stimulated. Glenn applied more and more strength from his horseback-riding-like stance.

"Heee! Oof! A-aghh, you're not done yet?!"

"Of course not. I've realized that the chiropractic treatment is even more effective on you than I imagined. It's possible that this won't just fix your crooked bones, but that it will preserve your body for a longer time. It looks like massaging is effective on flesh golems. If there was more data, I could write a thesis on the subject."

"You want to make me a guinea pig?!" Perhaps it was because she had been born as a result of a cruel doctor's experimentations, but the second she uttered that word, Kunai's body seemed to go completely stiff.

"No," Glenn answered without hesitation. "I am not a scholar. I am a doctor. Even if I were to collect data, your health would still be the most important thing. I would never let my priorities get so turned around that I only examined patients as a means to collect data."

"I-I see. Well, if you say so, I believe you."

"I will continue now," said Glenn.

"W-wait, I need to prepare myself. Mmmmwhoooooa?!"

Crackle, crackle.

Puff, puff.

The sounds were so loud that someone listening might have thought Kunai's bones were breaking.

"Heeee! Hee! Arggghh!"

Each time the bone moved closer to its proper place, Kunai let out a sound somewhere between a moan of pleasure and a scream.

Glenn decided to focus less on returning the bone to its original position and more on the relaxing effects of the massage.

"Mmmmm!"

"How are you doing?"

"Who cares how?! It's like I'm being shocked! In my back!"

"Please tell me if it's uncomfortable," Glenn warned.

"I-It's not uncomfortable... But!"

Then I can continue, thought Glenn.

Kunai's back already looked much better. Normally, Glenn wouldn't expect to see results after such a short amount of time. But it was more like he was adjusting the magic spell that held Kunai together, rather than adjusting her body.

"Ahh... Ahh... Are you done?" Kunai noticed that Glenn had let up.

"Yes. All finished."

She let out a strong sigh of relief. "Well… Thank you. I appreciate it." It sounded like she was trying to end the conversation.

"Miss Kunai, have you ever heard of acupuncture points?"

"What?"

Glenn was no longer on top of Kunai, so she sat up. He held out his hand to assist her.

"Acupuncture points are…pressure points, right?" Glenn asked. "I actually don't know much about them myself."

"Yes, acupuncture is a method of maintaining health by stimulating various pressure points on the body. It's often used in the east, and it was very common where I come from." Kunai was surprisingly knowledgeable on the subject.

Clearly, stimulating pressure points made the mind and body healthy and returned vitality to organs, but it wasn't possible to scientifically prove why this method was effective. Even when humans were dissected, no organs or apparatus like an acupuncture or pressure point had ever been found. Cthulhy had a certain understanding of pressure-point treatment, but she didn't include it in her monster medical practice. Pressure points were different for each monster, and it wasn't feasible to search out every pressure point for every species.

But.

Kunai resembled a human, and she was made up mostly of human parts.

"I would like to try something—may I?"

"But, my bone… It's fine now, right?"

"I discovered that massaging is effective for you, a corpse. That means that acupuncture points may be effective as well. Pressure-point treatment can be effective in alleviating fatigue."

"Hmmm..." Kunai wasn't sold, but Glenn was certain. He was sure that stimulating acupuncture points would improve Kunai's vitality. "Then...yes, please."

"Leave it to me. This time, please lie on your back."

"O-okay." Kunai rolled over.

Glenn sat by her legs and took off her pants. Kunai's legs were pale, and Glenn touched them gently. He could see all the way up to where her legs attached to her body. He draped a cloth across her waist to cover that region.

"Now, I will begin."

× ✖ ✖ ✖ ×

"Yeeooooowwwch!" Kunai let out a loud scream the moment the pressure point on her foot was pressed. It was not the kind of sound you would ever expect to hear from a warrior who had slain many beasts.

"Did that hurt?"

"Y-yes, it hurt! Idiot! I thought my sense of pain—aghh!"

Glenn had pressed on an especially significant pressure point as a test.

Kunai writhed in pain. In that moment, it was hard to believe she was a flesh golem, someone who didn't even flinch at a severed arm or foot.

"Eeeek, heee!"

"Hmm. That's strange..."

"It's not like I don't have any sense of pain. The reason I don't feel pain is because my magic is set up that way... This is... Aaargggggh!"

"I see. So, this is a different type of pain from what you were calibrated to block in the first place. Well, I'm sure they never anticipated pressure-point pain..."

"Don't keep going with that look on your face! Aaggghhhhh!"

It's said that pressure points affected each of the different parts in the body. The worse the state of the body part, the more painful the pressure point was when stimulated. In other words, the pain was proof that it was working. Kunai's body was dead, which meant that the state of her body was far from healthy. It also meant that she must have been in a lot of pain.

Kunai flapped her arms, showing just how much pain she was feeling.

"I-I said! Not so hard! Arrgh!"

"I'm not pressing hard," Glenn replied.

"L-Liar! Shut up! Eee!"

Each time Glenn pressed on one of the pressure points, Kunai bent backward. In truth, Glenn wasn't pressing that hard. But the bottoms of Kunai's feet were stiff, which meant that even weak stimulation was very effective.

"Grr! Hee! Aaaagh!"

"The pain is proof that it's working. Please bear with it."

"Th-this! I won't forget that you're doing this to me!"

Glenn was afraid of her taking revenge, so he tried pressing a bit harder. She arched her back, lifting her body off the ground as she stiffened against the pain. The cloth that had been covering her had already fallen to the ground from her flailing. Glenn could see her perfect chest jiggling from where he sat. The hem of her clothing had ridden up, and he could see glimpses of her panties. This wasn't good.

Glenn decided to try and finish as quickly as he could.

"Ooooooh... Th-this... I'm... By a man who isn't even a warrior..."

"It's nothing to cry about!"

"Idiot! Who is crying?! This is protective liquid for my eyeballs!" Kunai protested, trying to act strong.

Glenn was alone with a woman in this church. Moreover, her clothes were in disarray, and she was breathing hard and crying—well, according to her, it was protective liquid. What would Sapphee do if she found out?

He didn't want to think about it.

At the very least, Glenn wanted to fix the clothing that had come off from her squirming, but Kunai always wore such tight-fitting clothes. He'd have to touch her directly, and that was an ethical problem all on its own.

"Th-that's enough. Please, just finish..."

"But..."

"That's it. Isn't there a master pressure point that heals everything? If you use that, then you can finish right away, right?" Perhaps because she wasn't used to pain, Kunai spat the words out, flustered.

"Master? Well, yes, it does exist, but—"

"Then do it."

"Okay."

There was an acupuncture point that was effective for a wide variety of conditions. There was no reason for Glenn to hesitate at Kunai's request, but he didn't know if he should continue.

"Then, here we go."

"Wh—it's not on the bottom of the foot?"

"No. This pressure point is just below the knee. It's effective for recovering from exhaustion, strengthening your core, etc." Glenn searched for the pressure point with his fingers.

"U-umm, Dr. Glenn. Wait a second. I have a bad feeling about this."

"No, it's fine. This pressure point is extremely effective."

"Th-that's not what I mean—aaaaarrrghhhh!" She reacted as soon as he pressed on the pressure point. "Aghh! Oooooouchhhh!"

"Just as I thought, you're fatigued. I'm going to continue putting pressure on this point for three minutes."

"Th-three minutes?!" Kunai bit her lip to get through the pain. But even so, she couldn't help flailing her arms about.

"Stoppppp! It's too painfulllll!"

"It's okay, Kunai. Pressure points hurt, but in that pain is the proof that your mind and body are becoming healthier."

"Oooooh?! Are you...sure?!"

"Yes of course." Glenn pressed the point harder.

"Oooouchhhhh! That hurts!" She howled like a child. Her normal coolness was nowhere to be seen.

"Really? Isn't it starting to feel better yet?"

"Argh! Well, now that you mention it... Yes... Just a bit..."

It seemed like the pleasant feeling had only lasted a moment. But if she'd come this far, the rest was easy. All Glenn had to do was use his sensitive fingertips to find Kunai's pleasure point.

Even Glenn knew roughly where all the pressure points were. However, there were individual differences in the really effective pressure points, and only well-trained practitioners of acupuncture and moxibustion knew precisely where all of them were. Glenn had only a general understanding, but, somehow, he was able to find Kunai's points.

"Mmmm... Oof... Aaahh."

"It's already much better."

"N-no... It still...hurts. Mmm! B-but Ahh... There."

Her reaction had changed dramatically. Kunai's shoulders were trembling, and it seemed she didn't know how to react to the combination of pain and pleasure.

"Mmmmm. Hee, wooo!"

"That's right. I'll keep going." The three minutes were just about up.

"Ooh...mph, mm! Ahh..." Kunai's voice echoed flirtatiously in the church, empty but for the two of them.

This isn't the sort of thing that should take place in a church, Glenn thought. It would be fine to provide medical care in a church, but there was no way Kunai sounded like she was receiving treatment.

"Mmmmm! Mmm! Mmmmm..."

She was doing everything she could to stifle her voice, but her heavy breathing gave her away.

"Ahh... Ha... Aggh!"

"That's all, Miss Kunai. You're done... Miss Kunai?"

Kunai didn't show any sign of moving, even after Glenn stepped away. She was breathing hard. Her eyes were empty, staring off into space. Glenn called her name over and over, but she seemed to be in a trance.

"That felt...good..." Kunai muttered, not speaking to anyone in particular.

Perhaps she hadn't meant it for him, but Glenn heard her perfectly. The treatment had been more effective than he'd expected. He felt bad forcing her to get up, so Glenn left her where she was for a time. He did his best to avert his eyes from her chest and waist, where her clothes were coming off from all her wriggling around.

× × ✖ × ×

"Mmm... Mmm—" Kunai stretched both her arms as she stepped out of the church, looking very comfortable. "Hmm. My right arm—no, my whole body—feels lighter, like I've been reborn, even though I'm still dead." Kunai chuckled to herself.

She rotated her arms, checking her body. Thanks to Glenn's work, the new right arm had adapted itself to her body well.

"I'm happy to have aided in your recovery, Miss Kunai. I've now come up with the hypothesis that even a flesh golem made of corpses has vitality—the will to live."

"That's fine, but..." Kunai glared at him. "You'd better forget that I was howling with pain. It never happened. Forget it. If you mention it to anyone, the next place they'll see you is at the bottom of the canal."

"You'll upset the merfolk."

"Good-for-nothing doctor. You're worthless," she muttered.

It seemed like he had rekindled her hatred for doctors, even though her body had become lighter, meaning that the treatment had been effective.

"Well, it did feel kind of good..."

"Really? Then I'm glad I worked so hard."

"Shut up! Just a little! It's nothing! I was talking to myself!"

Glenn thought she was being irrational, getting angry so easily even though her body had benefited from the massage.

"I'll accompany you to the gate."

"Miss Kunai, you won't be returning to the town?"

"I have to put the arms away, and I also have managerial business to attend to. Those both come first."

"It's a lot of work to be acting manager."

"It's fine. It's necessary. The graveyard city was made based on my proposal, and I have no complaints about putting in the work to maintain it."

"Your proposal?"

"Ahh. Where should I start?" Kunai scratched her head and began talking as they walked. It was rare for her to speak about events from so long ago. "I was originally born in the east. I ran away from the doctor who created me and headed west, only because I didn't want to get caught. Luckily, I was created to be an undying soldier, so I didn't need food. I was a mess, but simply surviving was an easy task for me. I defeated all the beasts that tried to attack me and somehow ended up in Lindworm."

"..."

"At first, I lived as a fighter, but the Draconess saw my strength and selected me to be her bodyguard."

"Yes, I had heard that before..." Glenn interrupted.

"But that's just my public position." Kunai giggled, as if she were up to something. "Someone as strong as the Draconess doesn't need a bodyguard in the first place. She needed someone to keep watch while she was sleeping, so that was one reason for choosing a flesh golem like me..."

"But that wasn't all?"

"When I first met her, I had just entered the hall of fame and was being recognized at the arena. As I was receiving my certificate, the Draconess showed up. She asked me where I was staying."

It didn't make sense.

Induction into the hall of fame was an honor administered by the arena. Glenn didn't understand why Skadi would visit when Kunai was being bestowed that honor.

"That's the same expression I had when it happened."

Kunai laughed as she looked at Glenn. She often stood next to Skadi—who always had a serious look on her face—so it was refreshing to see her laughing so casually.

"I told her that I had been camping on the outskirts. I

explained that the residents would probably be frightened if they saw a patchwork corpse."

"That was—"

"Yes, at the time, the Draconess was trying to figure out what to do with the undead who were hanging around Lindworm. There were a lot of problems that needed to be considered if they were going to live with the other monsters. But ostracizing them would go against Lindworm's policy of becoming a town for humans and monsters to live in harmony."

Glenn nodded. Ever since Skadi became the City Council representative, Lindworm had accepted monsters from all over the mainland. There were also several monsters who had been living on the land for years, like Tisalia and Lulala. Creating a place for the undead to live comfortably was essential.

"I told her that it would be more comfortable if there was a base outside town. The Draconess accepted that, created the graveyard city, and appointed a manager."

"So, Skadi wanted someone close to her who could speak for the undead?"

"She didn't say it in so many words, but that's right. I'm grateful. I'm nothing but a corpse, yet she gave me a place to live, and a job. It's not only me, either. That's the case for most of the undead living here."

Glenn reflected on the fact that he hadn't known anything about the graveyard city until now. The living wouldn't normally have any reason to come to this place. But there was no question that the undead were *living* in this town.

"But without a manager, it goes nuts."

"I...see..."

"Yeah. The graveyard city wasn't like this before. Now it's full of miasma that creates spirits. We must do something quickly, or they'll break down the fence. If that happens, then some will spill outside. There's also a risk that some really scary things will try to get in and settle here..."

They could see the gate.

The day had been beneficial to Glenn—the town where the invisible spirits lived, the skeleton who reached nirvana, and the flesh golem in whom he'd aroused vitality. In the graveyard city, Glenn had seen life in a being without working organs, metabolism, flowing blood, or a heartbeat.

Kunai had called it the town that didn't need doctors. It was true that a doctor like Glenn was probably unnecessary in a town like this, but Glenn promised himself he would be back. Even if the graveyard city didn't need a doctor, he was sure he could learn much from the town that would prove useful in his practice.

Just then, Glenn remembered something; the one rumor that was spreading across Lindworm. Evil deeds. Spirits, perhaps.

"Oh, Miss Kunai. I have been wanting to ask you something."

"What is it?"

"Have any spirits left the graveyard town now that there's no manager on site? Have they maybe been causing a stir in Lindworm?"

"Oh, you mean the doppelgänger." Kunai nodded right away. It seemed like she knew exactly what Glenn was thinking. "Your concerns are well-founded. If the graveyard city got truly out of hand, I wouldn't be able to handle it on my own."

"N-no, that's not what I meant."

"But there are charms on the fence that surrounds the city. Wild ghosts can't get in, and once a spirit has come into the graveyard city, it becomes a resident. It can't go outside to do bad things. The old manager was a stickler for that sort of thing."

"But now...there is no manager..."

Kunai nodded, all too aware of this fact.

"I'm just a stand-in, but I'm doing my best to provide the minimum required management. The fence hasn't been broken yet, and I can say with certainty that no spirits have left. The doppelgänger commotion has nothing to do with the graveyard city."

"I see." Glenn was relieved to hear such a confident declaration.

His working theory was that the doppelgänger's true form was the heart he had removed from Skadi. However, if there were ghosts involved, that would upend all his logic. An incorporeal monster appearing in unexpected places at unexpected times could be explained by hallucinations. But, after hearing Kunai's words, Glenn rejected that theory.

Deadlich Graveyard City was a unique place, but there were people living here. It truly was a part of Lindworm, and Kunai valued this place as both a resident and its acting manager. Glenn felt bad for even thinking that a ghost might be the doppelgänger.

"I'll be going then."

"Yes. Thank you so much for today. Wait..."

"Huh?"

Kunai squinted her eyes, and a sharp sound cut through the air. Glenn felt cold wind on his face.

“This.” Kunai seemed to be holding something up high, but to Glenn it just looked like she was miming.

“Can you see it? There is a spirit here. It was trying to possess you.”

“Er.”

“Well, you are protected by the Draconess’s amulet, so it wouldn’t be able to possess you, but I’ll have to have some words with it for breaking its vow.”

“Oh, thank you,” Glenn said, bewildered. He wondered if spirits really could be caught with your bare hands. Or perhaps it was something Kunai could do because she was undead. “You caught it quickly. It looks like you’re already feeling better.”

“Thanks to your chiropractic and pressure points.”

“H-heh.”

Kunai grunted. She seemed to be twisting the ghost in her hands as if wringing out a towel. Glenn couldn’t see the spirit but felt like he could hear it screaming. After that, she tossed it away. He wondered if that kind of treatment was acceptable.

He changed his mind yet again. Even if they were residents of the graveyard city, they were still ghosts. You could never let your guard down when it came to them. Two had already tried to possess him in one day. If ghosts were to break out of the graveyard city and do whatever they wanted, the harm they would cause would far exceed what was happening with the doppelgängers. Skadi was right to appoint a manager.

"We have find a permanent manager as soon as possible."

"Is that something that can happen right away?"

"Apparently the Draconess has someone in mind. I wonder who it is. She hasn't even told me." Kunai looked off in the distance. Her gaze was fixed on the Vivre Mountains. Since the graveyard city was on a hill, there was a clear view of the towering peaks. "The Draconess is in the mountains now. I guess we'll see what happens..."

Glenn followed her gaze. He could see a dark shadow flying about halfway up the mountain. It could have been someone from the harpy village, which he had visited in the past.

He wondered what kind of person the former manager of the chaos that was Deadlich Graveyard City had been. The skeleton had been able to bring together the ghosts, control the undead, and govern the place as one town, so it couldn't have been an ordinary monster.

But that manager had already passed.

If only he could have met the skeleton and spoken with it. Maybe he could have learned more about the graveyard city. Glenn wavered between regret and desolation.

He closed his eyes for a moment and prayed that the manager, whose name he would never know, could rest in peace.

CASE 05:
The Gigas with Herculean Strength

SNAP.

Snap, snap.

"Aghhhh!"

The Giant Goddess—Dione Nephilim, a gigas—let out a pitiful scream.

"It brooooke agaaaain."

With a stature about ten times that of a human, Dione was the only survivor of the gigas race. She wasn't yelling to cause an earthquake—this scream was flat and lazy. There was still snow on the mountains.

Dione was curled up, still, but she was holding two small—well, small to a giant like Dione—tools.

"They're too smaaall."

Each time she raised her pitiful voice, the animals on the mountain gathered around. There were deer and goats by her feet and small birds resting their wings between the hairs on her head.

Wild rabbits pushed aside the snow to burrow in the warmth of her clothes.

Most surprising of all, the wolves, who would normally be eating those small animals, lay at Dione's feet, yawning instead of hunting.

Dione had a special air about her that calmed animals who would normally be subject to the law of the jungle.

"Ooohh, I'm so clumsy," she groaned as she tossed away the pencil she had been holding in her fingers.

It was a newfangled writing tool made from wood and graphite—a groundbreaking invention that didn't use ink, born from the development of graphite-processing technology. Pencils hadn't really become popular on the continent yet, but Lindworm tended to adopt new trends quickly and already had an established, independent trade route. A large shipment of pencils had come in recently. Sales were good, and more and more residents were taking to the tool.

But they were a bit… No, they were much too small for Dione.

"Ahhhhh. What a waaaaste."

There was a pile of broken pencils at Dione's feet.

According to Illy, so long as only the wooden shaft was broken, it could be remade at the workshop. But that was no excuse to waste so many brand-new products, especially since they'd just become popular.

The claim was that pencils were stronger than quill pens, which was why Dione had thought they might work for her. But it didn't matter if it was a pen or pencil, Dione's body was too big for them all.

She was bored.

The Giant Goddess Dione had too much time on her hands. It took days to reach the harpy village closest to the peak of the mountain, and her footsteps were always mistaken for earthquakes by those living there.

It was in Dione's nature to sit still. After the monster doctor, Glenn, had examined her, the residents of the village and an arachne woman had helped her take precautions against the frigid temperatures. She would never catch a cold again, even if she were covered in snow for 10,000 years.

Normally, she idled away the time, playing with the animals. Merchants would sometimes come to collect the precious ice that could only be found at the peak of the mountain, while other times, the youth from the harpy village would come bearing food offerings, but that was about it. Dione herself was as calm as a plant, but her life was unchanging.

She had decided to send for pencils so that she could correspond with her friends.

"I thought I could write a letterrrr."

She wanted to write to Skadi, Cthulhy, Glenn, the lamia woman, and the centaur woman. Oh, and the town elder she had known for a long time. And those young people she had just met. She thought it would be wonderful to hear what was going on in their lives, but...

"I can't do ittt."

The only ones who could hear her cries were the animals. The new wild boar sat at her feet and began snoring. There was no getting around it. Normal-sized pencils were just too small for Dione.

Snap, snap, snap.

Snap.

The pencils Dione had had delivered to the top of the mountain broke in half, one after another. At this rate, she would never be able to send any letters down to Lindworm.

"Aaaggghhh."

She sat curled up, hugging her knees.

In her hands was a small piece of paper and a small pencil.

Over the past few days, Dione had grown frustrated with trying to write. In that time, she'd only managed to write a few lines. What's more, her handwriting looked like a lamia had wriggled across the paper. It was illegible. This made the forlorn gigas want to break down and cry.

"Heeey!"

Dione thought she had heard a voice calling from far away. She lifted her head.

"Giaaant Godddessss!"

She looked up to the sky and saw a massive shadow. The colorful wings were way too big to be those of a bird, even a raptor, and they were far more exquisite than either the speaker's voice or the face, which told her exactly who it was.

It was Illy, a girl with some of the most beautiful wings in the harpy village.

"Yahoo, Giant Goddess!"

"Ohhh! Illy!" Dione was barely able to stop herself from waving her arms and instead just smiled at her friend.

If she were to wave her hands, it would make all the birds nesting on her head panic. Even if there hadn't been any birds, she always tried to minimize her movements.

Illy didn't have a last name. She'd been abandoned, and she'd never learned her parents' last name. She was just Illy. But she didn't mind one bit.

"Hey!" Illy landed on Dione's head with a grin on her face. "What's up, Giant Goddess? Oh, you've broken more pencils..."

"Ahhh. I'm sorry. After you brought them all the way up here."

"Well, I figured that would happen, so I brought you some more."

Once Illy showed up with her loud voice, the animals sensed danger and scattered all at once, back into the mountains. Even if they didn't find Dione to be a threat, they reacted like normal animals to Illy.

The package Illy held in her feet was full of pencils. She was busy delivering packages all over Lindworm as a courier for Scythia Transportation. Of course, Dione's mountain peak was part of her delivery route. Thanks to Illy's wings, it was easy to get to the top of the Vivre Mountains. Few people ever visited Dione, so the fact that Illy flew all the way up here to bring Dione packages and to chat meant that she was someone Dione could call a friend.

"Oh, Giant Goddess, I brought someone with me today." Illy flapped her wings over Dione's head.

"What?"

Someone else?

Unless it was another harpy, there weren't many who could fly to the mountain peak. There were very few monsters with flying abilities.

Illy collected the remains of the pencils that had been strewn about and put them in a bag, doing all of this with her feet. As she did, Dione tilted her head to the side, trying to imagine who the guest could be.

"Long time no see." A small shadow descended slowly.

Right in front of Dione's face, on top of the knees she was hugging with her arms, appeared a face that she knew well.

"Oooohh! Miss S-Skadiii!"

"Don't call me Miss, I'm the City Council representative."

"So whaaat? Heeey! I thought you weren't supposed to fly because you're siiick?"

"I had surgery, and I've recovered now, thanks to Dr. Cthulhy and Dr. Glenn."

"Oooh!"

Skadi Dragenfelt.

Dione had known the name for as long as Lindworm had existed. But she had only met Skadi in person a few times. Since they were both long-lived, she wanted to get to know Skadi better, but it wasn't easy for a dragon who couldn't fly and a gigas stuck on a mountain peak to find the time.

When she'd established the town, Skadi had come to greet Dione, but her face had been hidden by her robe, and she'd walked to the top of the mountain with many others. But now, the wings on Skadi's lower back were spread for flight. She had taken back the luxury of the skies.

"Wooow! That's amazing! Let me give you a big huggg!"

"Stop it this instant. I've only just recovered. If you keep it up, I'll fly away!" Skadi curled into a ball.

"You're a dragon, you'll be fine!" Illy joined in.

"That's enough out of you, Illy! Do you know how strong the Giant Goddess is?"

Dione hung her head in disappointment at being denied. "Ahhh... That's too baaad..."

Her body was too massive to express her affections without restraint. The world was too small for the gigas species to live in. That was why all the others of her kind had died off, leaving only Dione. It couldn't be helped, but it still made Dione feel sad. Her perspective on life and death was very different from that of humans, but she still felt lonely as the last of her kind.

That's why she was so happy that Illy and Skadi had come to see her.

"I'm glad to see you're doing well, Dione."

"Yesss, it's always the same for meee."

The gigas never changed or grew. Even though Dione had tried writing letters as a change of pace, it turned out the letters wouldn't grow either. Illy would probably take the broken pencils to the workshop to be repaired.

"Pencils aren't free, you know. Where do you think that money comes from?"

"Thank you so muuuch!" Dione couldn't bow her head, so she could only express her gratitude in words.

Illy always brought her pencils. The harpy never said anything, but Dione was sure that Skadi paid for them since Dione didn't have the means to pay for things. Even so, Skadi always made sure that she had ways to pass the time. Dione was glad for that.

"I know Illy is here on her delivery roundsss, but whyyy are you here, Skadi?"

"I just came to see your face, Dione."

"No waaay! You don't have time for that. Aren't you tired from flyiiing?"

"I thought you might notice." The look on Skadi's face said Dione was spot-on. Dione might live a carefree life, but even she knew that the City Council representative wouldn't come all the way to the peak of the mountain just to see her.

"You haven't heard of the doppelgänger...have you?"

"Of course I haaave."

"You probably wouldn't, way up here on the mountain—wait, you have?"

"The little birdies that fly around town told meee."

Illy, who had finished her task of collecting all the pencils, laughed.

She was the mail carrier for the town, in charge of letters, small packages, and newspapers. If it was within the weight limits, Illy could deliver anything in a jiffy. Of course, that meant that no rumor got past her. Illy was an important source of information for Dione, who couldn't go into town.

"I even saaaw it. It had turned into Memé."

"You did? That's true, there were reports of her." Skadi nodded. "In that case, I don't need to explain. The City Council is trying to track down the doppelgänger. It seems that it was also the fake heart that lived as a parasite in my chest."

"Oh nooo! Will you catch ittt?"

"Yes. If possible, I'd like to talk to it."

"That will beee tough!"

"You're acting as if it doesn't concern you."

Dione wasn't sure what Skadi meant. There wasn't much that Dione could actually do. She was worried that the doppelgänger was causing such a fuss in the town, but it wasn't as if she could down there—that would just cause more problems. The only things she could do were stay out of the way and hope for the best.

"The problem is that the doppelgänger understands the patrol team's movements and is cleverly avoiding them. We've put up a net in the canal, but we've only just begun, so we haven't caught it yet. The doppelgänger seems to be extremely intelligent."

"Oh myyy."

"Do you have any idea what the true form of this monster might be, Dione?"

"..."

Dione did have an idea.

The gigas weren't really gods, but they had once been called giant gods. Dione knew of several other species that were called gods in the same way. Dione's lifespan was longer than Skadi's, and Skadi was now putting that knowledge to use.

"Welll, it goes back to when Miss Cthulhy's ancestors were called malevolent gods and the like."

"So, thousands of years ago..."

"Yesss. Oh, but the ancestors of the scylla species weren't baaad. They just looked a bit scaryyy. But there were many storieees of them being kind to the gigasss."

"You're getting off track. What does this have to do with the... malevolent gods?"

"The subordinate of those malevolent gods—in other words, their aidddes—could change into anythinggg and do almost any kind of workkk."

"I had a feeling this was something from the distant past."

"They weren't just able to change fooorm. They were also thought to have significant knowledge and strength. And I've heard they have the ability to divide and multiplyyy."

"It sounds like they have a lot of similarities with the slimes..."

"Well, I've heard that when this particular species divides and multiplies, the leftovers actually become slime."

Skadi frowned.

Species that had lived for that long sometimes possessed such abilities. If this species had served the malevolent gods, then they'd been around much longer than Skadi—and even Dione. If they were causing the ruckus in Lindworm...Skadi couldn't even predict what would happen.

"Calling them a species is too vague. Can you think of anything else useful?"

"Aaah, well, I think they were called shoggoths?" She only had a vague memory of the name, but she was sure it was correct.

"Shoggoth... I'll remember that."

"Yesss." Dione smiled.

She was glad to be able to help Skadi, though it was unclear if the doppelgänger really was a shoggoth or not. Dione only knew the rumors that were flying about the town, and it wasn't her place to hypothesize as to what it really was. But if someone asked her for help, she would do what she could.

Dione couldn't move. Any movement, no matter how small, created problems for the animals, monsters, and humans around her, and she was far too soft-hearted to forgive herself for creating such a commotion. Skadi was aware of this, which was why she'd flown to the mountain peak, even as she was recovering from an illness.

"I wonder if shoggoths could live in the cityyy."

"We're not even considering that yet. First we need to figure out if they can even communicate."

"A species that can listen to the orders of the malevolent gods can probably have a conversaaation."

Dione hadn't moved from the peak of the mountain for a long time, and she didn't know any actual gods anymore, but she knew there were still species among the immature monster civilizations who worshipped 'gods'—giants and other such creatures. Even the dragons, like Skadi, were considered gods in some places. Dione may possess massive strength, but this continent was simply too small for a being like her to live on. Some gigas had gone to sleep deep in the ocean, while others had created their own realms in the sky to hide themselves. Even Skadi's dragon ancestor had run away to their holy precincts. No matter where they were born, the shoggoths had to be kindred spirits to Dione and Skadi. They came from a time when the gods were common and familiar.

There was no way they couldn't converse.

"They would do fiiine in Lindworm."

Even the doctor who'd examined Dione's cold had never thought she couldn't talk simply because she was a giant. And though she seemed to break everything with even the smallest of movements—how many pencils had she broken just trying to write a letter?—Skadi and Illy never treated her like a god, either. There was no one left who would even think to call her a god. Well, the harpies still called her "Giant Goddess," but they didn't mean it in a bad way, so she didn't stop them. She didn't want to be a god, she just wanted to be a normal monster...

And, if possible, she also wanted the shoggoths to become one of Lindworm's resident monster species.

Ohhh, but...

Dione stared at Skadi with eyes hidden behind her hair. According to Skadi, the doppelgänger had been living off her for many years. Skadi wasn't the type to dwell on petty things, so she might forgive it easily. But even if she did, would the residents of Lindworm be so forgiving?

"Can I give you one piece of adviiiice?"

"Go ahead."

"I'm sure the shoggoths' understanding of the current world is inferior to oooours. They've only ever served the malevolent gods..."

"So what?"

"They may have knowledge and intelligennnce...but when it comes to morality and ethics, they could be verrry immatuuure. Maybe even more immature than a child."

The fact that the doppelgänger had mimicked Skadi's heart was a prime example. While it was still a mystery *why* it had infested Skadi, the result was that it had nearly killed her. Generally, parasites only killed their hosts when they'd found another one and were ready to move on...

Did that mean the doppelgänger had had another host lined up for itself after it killed Skadi?

No... Dione thought. *No body would be as rich a host as a dragon's. It hasn't thought that far ahead.*

Since Dione couldn't move, she had a lot of time on her hands. She'd had time to collect everything she'd heard from Illy up to now, consider all the angles, and contemplate. It might appear that she lazed around, even seeming ditzy at times, but she actually did possess the wisdom worthy of being called a god.

"It doesn't have any sense of reasoning, so it may cause damage even without meaning tooooo. The fact that Skadi almost died is proof of thaaaaaat."

"There have still been no reports of a doppelgänger attacking anyone."

"Yes, well, perhaps it feels baaad about what it did."

Shoggoths were supposed to have a high capacity for learning. If the doppelgänger were to hurt someone, Skadi and the patrol team would track it down relentlessly. If it came to that, they wouldn't try to take it into protective custody or apprehend it—the orders would be to destroy it. Dione wondered if the doppelgänger understood that much. Even if shoggoths didn't have a sense of reason, the doppelgänger seemed like it was making efforts to understand other monsters. Maybe that was why it was changing into various forms. If it were transforming to learn...

What would happen if, once it was done learning, it decided that it was fine to hurt other monsters?

"Pleeease be careful. I've heard that people who meet their doppelgänger diiie."

"I know that. But isn't that because ghosts and phantoms show them an illusion? A ghost possesses someone and shows them a hallucination of something that's not real. Then the person possessed by the evil spirit gets weaker and weaker... That's what made everyone think that if you saw your doppelgänger you would die."

"Maybe that's not aaall."

"Do you know something?"

"I don't know anything. But, the rumor of doppelgängers has spread throughout the towwwn. It feels like the tales of dying when you see your doppelgänger might come truuue. Wouldn't that be horrrrible?"

Of course, this was nothing more than a gut feeling Dione had. But it was enough to make Skadi more alert. The Draconess was quiet for a moment, then she spread the wings on her lower back.

"Thank you for your help, Dione."

"Nooo problem. Please come see me agaaain."

"If I feel like it," Skadi said curtly.

But Dione had a feeling she would be back. Once Skadi had regained her ability to fly, the first place she went was this mountain peak. She would probably come again unexpectedly.

"Okay then, Giant Goddess. I'll be going too," said Illy, as she spread her wings. She had collected all the broken pencils.

Illy was impatient. She and Dione got along well, but the way they used their time was completely different. Illy's tendency was to hurry up and finish whatever was in front of her. If you looked away for even a second, she would already be on her way back to Lindworm.

Dione found herself flustered. She stretched out her arm. "Waaait!"

"Arrrgh!"

Dione grabbed Illy by the neck with her fingers, like she was catching a dragonfly. The difference in their physiques was enormous, and Illy was struggling.

"Aaah! What?!"

Dione had startled Illy. This happened sometimes when she moved, even if she moved without the intention of harming anyone. She was better off staying still.

"Ummm. Sorryyy. I have a favor to aaask."

"Huh?"

"I want you to deliver a letter for me."

"You do?" Illy put on her serious courier face. Once she heard the word "letter," she couldn't stay silent. She slipped out of Dione's hand, landing on the ground. "No problem! I'll deliver it wherever you want!"

"Thank youuuu. I'm going to write it nooow."

Dione picked up paper and a pencil. She had already decided what to write. It was about the doppelgänger, and how important and necessary it was for Lindworm to be the kind of town that welcomed any monster. It should be easy to turn that into a letter.

Dione made up her mind and gripped the pencil.

"Ummm."

She put the pencil to the paper, determined to write.

Snap.

"Aaaahh."

It was no use. There was nothing that could be done.

Pull yourself together and try again. She grabbed another pencil and wrote one letter.

Snap.

Snap, snap. Snap.

"Oooooooh."

Snap, snap, snap.

Snap.

When she had wasted about ten pencils, Illy spoke up.

"Ummm... Giant Goddess? I have to make deliveries this afternoon, so I need to be going."

"Ohhhhhh."

"I'll come back this evening, okay?"

"I-I'm sorryyy..."

Even though Dione still had a lot of extra pencils, at this rate, it would take her an entire day just to write one letter. She didn't even know if she could finish it. But it was vital for Dione to write the letter, and for Illy to deliver it, as quickly as possible.

"I-I'll do my beeest! I'll try harder than I have at anything in the last one thousand yeeears!"

"Okay! I'll be waiting!" Illy, with her infinite cheerfulness, laughed as her crimson wings sparkled in the afternoon sun.

Apparently, Illy used to mope a lot, but it was hard to imagine that looking at her today. The young harpy girl flapped those brightly colored wings and flew off to Lindworm. Whenever she had time between deliveries, she flew to the mountain peak. She'd become an irreplaceable part of Dione's life.

Now then.

"Let's goooo!"

Dione. The clumsy Giant Goddess. The one who brought nothing good when she moved. Even so, it was important for her to move her hand now. She held the pencil—which to her was the equivalent of a tiny needle in human terms—and began writing her letter. But as soon as she grew too excited—

Snap.

"Oooohhhh!"

The Giant Goddess let out a pitiful wail.

Some rabbits hopped around her feet, as if to comfort her.

She did finish that day.

Surrounded by animals, Dione finally managed to write the letter she needed to hand off to Illy. The words were scrawled out in the continent's official language, the common tongue. They looked like wriggling lamia, and there were probably some old phrases mixed in that would be hard to understand, but Dione believed that the recipient of the letter would be able to decipher it, so she entrusted it to Illy.

She believed that her thoughts, collected on the top of a mountain she couldn't move from, needed to be delivered.

CASE 06:
The Mermaid with a Twin

THE DIVA of the central plaza, the mermaid Lulala Heine, had just woken up.

Lulala's eyes opened to the morning light streaming into her underwater home. Her bedroom décor included a modern bed made from a giant clamshell and a waterproof arachne mattress. It was extremely luxurious—worth ten coins—but this clamshell ensured she slept soundly.

"Mmmm. Morning already?"

Lulala's two sisters were in the clamshell with her.

Lulala was the oldest of five children. She had two younger sisters and two younger brothers. The rent for Lulala's house was cheap, so they didn't have a lot of room. A bedroom for each child was a luxury they couldn't afford.

"Remy, Soula, hurry! Wake up!"

"Mmmaah."

"Just five more minutes."

"No. Go help Mom."

"Glub, glub." Both of Lulala's sisters let out bubbles of protest as they left the clamshell bed.

Once she had them out of the room, Lulala began swimming. When merfolk slept, they were essentially naked. Traditionally, it was normal for both mermaids and mermen to spend their lives naked. Clothes only got in the way in the water, so there was no need for them to hold to the same customs as the women, men, and monsters on land.

But nudity wouldn't fly in Lindworm.

The underwater clothing made by the arachne had recently become quite popular among the merfolk. Furthermore, if Lulala didn't wear a bathing suit when she sang in the central plaza, not only would people judge her, but it would reflect on all the merfolk living in the Waterways.

More than anything, Lulala was embarrassed to show her chest in front of men.

She hadn't had this sense of shame in the sea. It was something she'd developed only after living in the city, though she still didn't mind being naked among her own people.

Lulala put on her waterproof garment, made from a triangular piece of cloth, and a mesh skirt. She could worry about her accessories, made from merrow glass, later.

"Okay!"

She was still a bit sleepy.

Lulala slapped her cheeks, ready to begin the day.

The morning sun was growing brighter and brighter in the canal.

× × × × ×

Breakfast was a feast: freshwater squid wrapped in waterweed, fish-meat sausage stuffed in shrimp shells, and several freshly caught river fish. Each of the small dishes were lined up on the table, which was made from a sea turtle shell. Lulala didn't think they'd be able to eat so much in one morning. She gave her a mother a look.

"M-mother, what is this?"

"Hehehe. A man at the market said he got a big catch today." Lulala's mother was grinning. She'd probably gotten a good deal.

Lindworm was far from the ocean, so most of the fish were caught in the Vivre River. Fish were one of merfolk's main food sources, and the river contained a wide variety. In one area of the river, there was even a breeding ground where waterweed, shellfish, shrimp, squid, and octopus were grown for food. River fish weren't generally eaten on the mainland because they smelled and went bad quickly, but that wasn't an issue for merfolk. Fish tasted the best when they were freshly caught and served raw with seasonings.

The foods merfolk ate were very different from those eaten by land dwellers. Generally, merfolk didn't cook. They also didn't eat liquids, like soups or sauces. They loved natural, freshly caught seafood.

"I want sausage!"

"Hey! I was gonna eat that!"

"Finders keepers, Van!"

"Syd! You'll make Soula cry again!"

"She's fine. The waterweed squid is good! Om-nom-nom."

"Lulala! Can I have seconds?"

"Syd, don't eat so much! Make sure everyone gets their share."

The growing children had healthy appetites, and all their favorite foods were lined up on the table. Some said that merfolk couldn't cook, but if you asked Lulala, just heating something up over a fire wasn't cooking. Merfolk were skilled at making foods delicious, even underwater.

Lulala loved eating the shrimp-shell sausage, shell and all. She looked at her mother as she took a bite. Her mother looked happy surveying the lively dining table.

"Mom?"

"Oh—sorry. I think I might cry."

"Why, did I do something?"

"No Lulala. It's just...I don't think we've ever eaten like this before. Ever since you started singing in the plaza and earning money, everyone has been eating well. Syd, Remy, Van, and Soula, and you, of course. I made you suffer so much before."

"Don't cry! You're so dramatic."

Lulala's mother worked harder than anyone. The family had originally lived in the sea, but, one day, their father suddenly told them they would be moving to the new Waterways. But his business there didn't go well, and he soon found a new woman and returned to the ocean. Lulala didn't harbor any anger toward him, or his failure at being a father, but she did wish he'd at least left them some money. In that way, Lulala was a realist.

In that way, she thought, she was unlike her mother.

Her mother had light skin and delicate features. She was thin for a mermaid, perhaps because she was from a deep part of the ocean. She was more like the merfolk in fairy tales. Lulala's skin was tanned, and she was envious of her mother's fair complexion. She also wished she'd inherited her mother's graceful and composed mannerisms.

"Lulala, you'll be home late tonight, right?"

"Yes, today is the celebration for Tisalia's promotion."

"Well, have fun! And don't drink too much!"

"This is work, Mother!" Lulala raised her voice. Her mother seemed to think she was going out to have a good time.

Tisalia had recently been promoted to rank two, so Kay and Lorna had called all of Tisalia's friends to a celebration at the Giant Squid's Inn. She wondered how many people in the town would come to a celebration for the sole daughter of Kimmeria and Hephthal Scythia. Sapphee, the lamia from the clinic, would probably stop by. No matter what they said, she got the feeling Sapphee and Tisalia were close.

And if Sapphee were there, then Dr. Glenn would be too...

"Got it!"

"No!"

Her brother Syd was trying to take her waterweed wrap. Lulala stopped him by quickly slapping his hand away. Syd always tried to take things from people. As his older sister, she needed to discipline him properly.

"When will you guys be done eating? Don't you have work to do?!"

"Yessss!" they all answered in unison.

Syd was apprenticing as a sailor; Remy worked on decorations for the canal parade; and Van helped out at the gondola stall. Now that everyone had a place to work, the Heine household's circumstances had improved significantly. The youngest, Soula, stayed home and helped their mother.

There was a saying, *There is no leisure for the poor*. The truth was that, as a family of six, they were still struggling.

Lulala was the breadwinner, and as the oldest sister, she disciplined her younger siblings strictly. While she had gained popularity as the diva of the central plaza, she still didn't make nearly as much as the more experienced divas in the canal.

I need to work harder...

"Okay, I'm leaving now, Mother."

Lulala put on her merrow glass accessories and was ready to go.

"You're going so early?"

"It's not *that* early. I have to greet the madam at the inn, too. And I have a meeting with the orchestra. Goodbye!"

Lulala's home was a series of ruins that had been rebuilt for the merfolk, sunken at the bottom of the canal. The inside was protected from the strong current, but once Lulala swam outside, she found herself on a one-way path full of aquatic monsters. Lulala's mother and siblings saw her off as she disappeared into the crowd.

She stuck out her tongue just a little as she swam.

Lulala took out a sausage she had hidden in her skirt and felt only a little guilty for hiding it from her family. She headed not toward the Giant Squid's Inn, where she would be working today, but to the deserted No. 4 canal.

She had lied. She didn't need to be at work so early.

As she swam closer to Canal No. 4, she saw fewer and fewer monsters.

But...

Lulala had important business to attend to that day.

"Ptooey!"

When Lulala arrived at a dead end at the edge of Canal No. 4, she poked her head above the surface of the water. The moment she did, her body switched from branchial to pulmonary respiration. She spit the excess water out of her mouth and began breathing air. Lulala had almost died from a respiratory disease once but had recovered thanks to Glenn's treatment.

Canal No. 4 wasn't used often. Since it was a dead end, and because there was a sewer nearby, there were no stalls and very few tourists. In the Merrow Waterways, the sewage canals and the residential canals were strictly separated, but there was no way to mask the unpleasant smell in the air. As a result, land dwellers never passed by Canal No. 4.

So, why had Lulala come this far?

"Hello? I'm here."

The merfolk language was specialized for speaking underwater, so when Lulala was on land, she used the official language of the continent. Before Lulala even knew whether the *thing* could understand language, she had repeatedly tried speaking to it. It seemed to somewhat understand the official language.

The *thing* was sitting motionless in one corner of the canal's dead end. As far as Lulala knew, it never moved from this spot. But she didn't think it was incapable of moving.

"Were you a good girl?"

Lulala spoke to the *thing* as if it were a child.

It didn't reply to her, but after some time, it nodded.

So, it does *understand the official language.*

The *thing* was Lulala.

"I only brought a little. It's raw, but do you think you can eat it?"

"..." The *thing*—a young girl with Lulala's face—nodded in response to her question.

The *thing* took the shrimp-shell sausage Lulala had brought for it. At first, it just stared at it, but, eventually, it put it in its mouth.

Lulala didn't know what the *thing* liked to eat, but it finished all the seafood she brought from home. It never complained, so Lulala figured it was probably fine. Probably.

It was the doppelgänger that everyone in town was talking about.

It really concentrates when it eats, Lulala thought as she watched this *thing* with the same face as her.

She had heard the rumors: people saying they saw something that looked exactly like someone they knew. But Lulala never thought it would appear with her own face.

"Hey, if you're going to mimic me, make sure you mimic my beautiful singing voice too."

"………"

The doppelgänger said nothing. It looked exactly like Lulala, but there were two differences, one being that it didn't talk. It seemed to understand language, but it never spoke.

The second difference was obvious if you looked at its lower body. There were no scales or tail like you would find on merfolk. Instead, it had grown two human legs.

That's right, the other Lulala was completely human.

"You're not going to mimic me exactly? That's weird." Lulala splashed the water forcefully with her tail.

She jumped out of the water with the skill of a dolphin and sat on the stone street. *If someone saw us sitting here together with the same face, it would certainly cause a fuss,* she thought.

Two weeks had passed since she first met the thing. Lulala had just happened to have some extra time, and she ended up in Canal No. 4. There weren't a lot of people here, but sometimes copper coins flowed down this way. Tourists from the main waterway dropped things, and they ended up at the end of the waterway. Lulala hadn't been able to break the habit of searching for change from back when she was poor.

The first time she met the doppelgänger, it didn't have Lulala's face. So, whose face had it been? She couldn't describe it. It looked like someone she knew. It looked both male and female. It was a face with a mysterious composition, like an illusion. But Lulala, who liked to care for things, couldn't leave it alone.

The doppelgänger hadn't run away like she'd heard in the rumors. It just seemed forlorn. After their first meeting, Lulala went home to collect some food for it. When she came back, the doppelgänger had already changed its face to look exactly like her. It was just like staring into a mirror.

Lulala had met the thing many times since then. The biscuit she'd received from Lorna went to the doppelgänger, which happily gobbled up the homemade treat—or at least, it looked that way.

"I don't know what your situation is, but you'll feel better if you eat something."

"..."

The *thing* nodded.

It seemed timid, or maybe lacking in self-confidence, which reminded Lulala of her mother and little sister, Soula. Perhaps that was why she couldn't just leave it alone.

"You ate it all up. Were you hungry?"

"..." The *thing* nodded.

"I don't know how long I can keep bringing you food. You need to search for things to eat on your own... But you don't have any clothes. I guess you can't go out to the city like that."

"..." Another nod.

"Hmmmm. I could ask Arahnia. But—"

"...?"

The doppelgänger was unexpectedly friendly. Even though it didn't talk, it stared intently at Lulala, changing its facial expression in response to her words. It seemed especially interested in hearing about Lulala, her family, and the women she admired, Sapphee and Arahnia.

"Tell me, why do you have legs?"

"...?"

"Don't you know any fairy tales? The little mermaid traded her voice for legs. Then she went to meet the man she loved."

"..." The *thing* shook its head.

"If I were the little mermaid, I would probably look like you."

"..."

The man she loved.

The man Lulala loved...was the man who'd saved her when she nearly drowned. It wasn't like they were separated by the gulf between land and sea. She saw him sometimes in the central plaza, so she didn't need to sacrifice the voice she was so proud of to get legs. Even so, when she saw the doppelgänger with human legs, she couldn't help but imagine.

"Ugh!"

A fantasy was playing out in her head. Lulala had become human and was walking through the shopping street in Lindworm, arm in arm with Dr. Glenn. When she cried out, the image disappeared.

"Ugh! Ugh!"

"..." The *thing* looked around frantically.

Seeing an emotionally unstable Lulala flustered the doppelgänger. It couldn't do anything for her, even though the entire reason it had taken on that form was because of Lulala's anguish. It wasn't like Lulala to push her troubles onto someone she didn't know.

Still, Lulala hoped she could find a way. Saphentite was a lamia, but she liked Glenn all the same. Marriage between humans and monsters was legal in Lindworm, and there were many inter-species couples. It wasn't impossible simply because Lulala was a mermaid.

"So, what are you going to do now?"

"..."

"Do you want to find Miss Kunai? She'll talk to Skadi for you. Or maybe it's better to go to Tisalia? They take in orphans at the mansion. Ah, but maybe that's only centaur orphans. That won't do."

"..."

"Come on! Say something!" Lulala laid her hands on the stone.

The doppelgänger narrowed its eyes as if it were thinking about something, but it didn't speak. Perhaps the second Lulala, whose voice had been stolen by the sea witch, couldn't speak even if it wanted to.

"Today, there's a celebration for Miss Tisalia."

"..."

"Miss Sapphee will be there, and Miss Arahnia too. But I'm sure all of them...like Dr. Glenn."

Dammit! thought Lulala.

Glenn Litbeit was a desirable man. What's more, he was sought after by many monster women. The reason was clear: No matter what kind of monster, he always did everything he could to save them. And he never looked more handsome than when he was intently administering treatment.

Lulala's specialty was love songs. Perhaps that's why she was especially sensitive to signs of love.

"..."

"Hmm? What?"

The doppelgänger was patting Lulala on the shoulder, of its own accord. That had never happened before. Lulala had almost never even seen the doppelgänger move on its own. Whenever she met the doppelgänger, she gave it food, and, in exchange, the doppelgänger listened to all her complaints. But now the fake Lulala was patting her shoulder gently.

She found it encouraging.

After the doppelgänger had been patting her for some time, she realized that she longed to receive that kind of support from someone. All she did was sing in the central plaza—songs for people's safety, love, and life. That was Lulala's job, and she enjoyed it. She could even make a living at it, so she didn't want to complain, but...

Oh.

The reason she talked to this doppelgänger, who did nothing but nod, was because she wanted strength. The strength to sing for people.

"Hmmm... Thank you."

"..." The doppelgänger smiled.

It was the same smile she'd seen so many times in her reflection. But it felt...different. For the first time in her life, she understood just how encouraging a smiling face could be.

Strange.

This doppelgänger had the city in an uproar and everyone scared, but to Lulala, it was a comforting companion.

"Okay! I feel a lot better. Maybe it's time to sing!"

"...?"

"Don't worry, it's fine. I have to sing at the inn today, so I need to warm up my voice first. No one else will hear me here. It's rare for me to sing for just one person."

"..." The doppelgänger nodded.

"What should I sing? A rhapsody? An aria? A requiem? Since it's a special occasion, maybe I should do a medley?"

She knew just the medley.

Lulala sang; she sang from her heart. She sang various types of songs, believing it was the best way to show how she was feeling.

The doppelgänger smiled and clapped its hands as it listened.

"Hmm..."

Lulala's throat was in perfect condition. Her gills were fine too. She was sure work would go well today. Even if she was unsure about love, she was sure she could do great things as a performer, no matter what.

"Thank you. I'll come back after I'm done with work."

"..." The doppelgänger nodded.

It wasn't as if Lulala never thought about what she was, why she was here, or how she'd ended up in this situation, but none of that really mattered to her. Today, in this moment, as she and the doppelgänger smiled at each other—like smiling into a mirror—she knew for sure that she had gained a best friend.

Apparently, Lulala didn't have very high standards when it came to choosing friends.

That night, things went just like the rehearsal.

"—————————♪"

Lulala sang with everything she had, filling the Giant Squid's Inn with her voice. She sang a traditional waltz from the western side of the continent, singing it with all her heart, accompanied by the orchestra. She sang with all her might, directly to Tisalia, who was sitting on the balcony.

The Giant Squid's Inn had a kraken madam and a small terrace seating area that reached to the canal. An impromptu stage had been constructed, just for the day, and Lulala sat on a chair, with half her body in the water. The orchestra was made up of people who performed in pubs around town as well as the Waterways parade. Their music blended well with Lulala's voice.

Lulala sang with all her ability, and the performance was perfect.

When she finished singing the waltz, the crowd broke out in applause.

"That was amazing!"

The first one to say it was the guest of honor, Tisalia. Her hooves clip-clopped as she ran to the waterway, nearly knocking Lulala over with her greeting.

"Lulala, that song you sang for me was so amazing! Thank you so, so much!"

"Heh... Congratulations on your promotion, Miss Tisalia!"

"Ohh, hohoho! Feel free to praise me as much as you want tonight! The arena has finally seen what I can do!" It was just like Tisalia not to show any modesty here.

She stood out from the crowd, adorned in her beautiful dress. And whenever she laughed loudly, her guests called out things like, "That's great, my lady!" and "I knew you could do it, Princess!"

"B-but, Miss Tisalia, you've really gone all out today."

When Lulala pointed this out, Tisalia's face grew red.

"Uh."

The bust of Tisalia's dress was wide open. It was only held on by a string tied around her neck. Most of her back was also exposed. As usual, her hair was up in a bun, baring the nape of her neck as well. Lulala blushed just from looking at her.

"Oh, this... Kay and Lorna... Um, well... Don't look..."

"What are you saying, my lady? You'll never use those in battle. This is your chance to get some use out of them!"

"Don't say such things!"

Seeing Tisalia in a dress like that, which showed off her impressive cleavage, Lulala knew that there was no way she—or anyone—could compete for Glenn's attention. That must have been part of Kay and Lorna's plan when they selected the dress. To someone as small as Lulala, this realization was like a punch to the gut.

In terms of exposure, Lulala's water clothing matched Tisalia's, but she wasn't even on the same scale when it came to her bust.

"Let's stop talking about this! Lulala, come over here. There are still plenty of the madam's delicious dishes left. Kay, Lorna! Show the diva where the food is."

"You're changing the subject from your naked body?"

"My lady, to secure the doctor's admiration—"

"That's enough! It's just as important to show the diva a good time!"

"Yes, my Lady."

"This way, Miss Lulala."

"Okay!" Lulala jumped out of the canal and slid on her belly across the stone terrace. Her movements looked like that of a seal, but merfolk could move quite quickly over the ground in this manner.

She squirmed up onto a chair. Salted caviar on crackers were spread out in front of her.

"Don't mind if I do!" Lulala had had her eye on the most expensive dish in the venue ever since she'd started singing.

It was a celebration worthy of the famous Scythia Transportation, a name that resounded throughout the continent. The table was full of food made from ingredients found in the sea where Lulala was born, which made her nostalgic. She also felt a little guilty eating without her family, but the food was part of her payment, so she ate to her heart's content.

The terrace of the inn was covered with a massive awning to keep out the rain. The framework of the awning made it look like a giant squid's legs were holding it up. It wasn't clear if the awning had been made to match the name of the inn, or if the inn was named for the awning.

Lulala looked around as she ate her caviar and crackers. Since it was a celebration for the heir of Scythia Transportation, there were many centaurs in attendance. But there were also some other familiar faces.

"Umm... Miss Tisalia?"

"Oh, is everything alright? Are you having trouble eating something?"

"No, it's not that... There are a lot of people here, huh?"

"Yes, we invited everyone we see regularly. Memé from the workshop makes my armor and our practice spears, Arahnia makes the cloth parts, and though it was only a formality, we invited the City Council representative as well."

"What? What did Miss Skadi have to do with your promotion? Some kind of backroom deal?"

"We would never do something like that! It's hard to explain, but there's a deep connection..."

"...?" Lulala cocked her head to one side.

There was no way for Lulala to know that Skadi had interfered the day Tisalia was promoted. Tisalia mumbled, "Oh, and we know each other from the clinic, too."

"Oh, yes, I knew about that."

"How in the world am I going to get this home?" Tisalia was looking at a giant frame.

Inside the frame was...a snake? No, it was the exuvia of a lamia. As far as Lulala knew, Tisalia was good friends with only one lamia. In the corner of the frame, it said, "Congratulations on your promotion. From, Litbeit Clinic."

"W-wow, a lamia exuvia..."

"At first, I thought it was a prank. I mean, lamia exuviae are highly coveted as good luck charms. And I don't know where I could display it in the company offices..."

She was complaining, but the fact that Tisalia was even thinking about displaying it meant that she must have really liked Sapphee. Also, the fact that Sapphee had put her own flawless exuvia in a frame was also a sign of friendship. It must have taken a lot of effort for Sapphee to shed it. But the contributor of the gift was nowhere to be seen.

Lulala looked around the room. Generally, wherever Sapphee was, Glenn would be close by. While Lulala searched for Sapphee, she also looked for Glenn.

"She ordered some expensive wine too. Where did that serpentess run away to?"

Lulala's heart beat faster. Had Tisalia read her thoughts? Or noticed her yearning for Glenn? Tisalia probably wasn't the jealous type, even if she *had* noticed. But if she were to discover how awkward Lulala was when it came to love, even though she sang so many love songs, it would be embarrassing, to say the least. Lulala wished she could leave her feelings for Glenn at the bottom of the canal whenever she came up on land.

Ahh.

That made her remember the doppelgänger. It was probably still in the corner of the canal. She wished it could hold onto her yearning for her.

"Who are you calling a 'serpentess'?" Sapphee suddenly appeared, patting Tisalia on the back of the neck.

"Heeee?!" Tisalia screamed and nearly jumped out of her own skin. "Hey... Ugh! What are you doing?! You smell like alcohol!"

"It's an open bar."

"Go ahead, get your drink on! But if you pass out, I'm not carrying you home!"

"Have I ever passed out before? Oh, good evening, Miss Lulala." Sapphee took a glass of wine from a nearby waitress with her tail. Lulala wondered how much more she was going to imbibe, given how clearly drunk she was already. Sapphee liked to drink.

"Weren't you the one singing?" Sapphee smiled at Lulala, completely ignoring Tisalia's guffaw. "That waltz was perfect for me!"

Lulala thought of Sapphee as a sweet older sister, and she knew Sapphee felt the same way. She'd been kind to Lulala when her gills were damaged, and since then, Lulala had seen her a few times for various reasons. Yet, even though Sapphee was in a position Lulala should respect, she always felt uneasy around the lamia for some reason. And whenever she saw Sapphee, she looked around in hopes that Glenn would be with her.

"Oh, where is the doctor?" Tisalia said what Lulala had been thinking.

It seemed all the girls wanted the same thing.

"Well, he...ummm."

"What is it? It's not like you to slur your words."

"He was with me until not too long ago... Then he said he was going to see Lulala."

"Huh?" Sapphee cocked her head to the side and looked at Lulala.

Coming to see her? But Lulala hadn't seen Glenn at all that night. She had been looking for him ever since she got to the Giant Squid's Inn. If she had seen him, she would have spoken to him.

"Maybe he missed you?" Tisalia jumped in. "But you were singing here the entire time. I don't see how that's possible."

"Maybe he went to the central plaza?"

"What?" This time, Tisalia cocked her head to the side as if she had no idea what was going on. Lulala felt the same way.

"But...why?"

"If I knew that, we wouldn't be having this conversation. He was muttering about something, saying that he wasn't going to be able to have any fun at the party, so I left him."

"Y-you... Do you have any idea how I felt when I invited him?! And this embarrassing dress that I'm putting up with... You mean to say he's not coming?!"

"Settle down, Tisalia."

"How can I settle down?! Oh, Doctor... When I invited him, he promised he'd come... Am I really that unimportant to him?!"

"I told him that you wanted him to celebrate with you. He said he'd definitely stop by later..."

"You better be telling the truth! I'm trusting you, Sapphee!"

"Please don't get upset. The doctor will come, so long as he hasn't forgotten." Sapphee took another drink of wine.

Lulala wondered if it was okay for her to drink so much. Merfolk didn't drink alcohol, so she didn't really understand the appeal.

She had a bad feeling. *Going to meet...me?* She'd been at the inn the entire time.

The inn wasn't that far from the central plaza. Surely, by now, he would have discovered she wasn't there and returned.

Lulala remembered something. The *other* Lulala.

But how could Dr. Glenn know about her...

She didn't know, but she was sure about one thing: If Glenn saw the doppelgänger, even with its human legs, he would definitely think it was Lulala. It had the exact same face as her. Even Lulala thought so.

"But I'm here," Lulala said.

She decided to laugh out loud. Even when her gills were swollen and her throat was sore, Lulala sang with everything she had. And she never stopped smiling. So...she was fine, so long as she kept smiling.

Lulala felt a sharp pang of anxiety in her chest, like she was being stabbed with a knife. But hiding that sort of feeling was her specialty.

"That's so strange. What was the doctor thinking?"

"Seriously." Sapphee drained her wine glass and let out a sigh. "The doctor was...strange today. I wonder if it was really him."

"Huh?"

"Maybe it was the doppelgänger..." The lamia laughed, as if she were joking. If Sapphee couldn't tell whether Glenn was real, then no one could.

Lulala thought back to when she'd lived in the sea.

The sea was bottomless. As a child, Lulala had once swam so far away that she sank into an abyss where no sunlight could reach. She'd been chasing after beautiful fish and had forgotten about the depth. But she immediately knew she was in an abyss by how cold it was. In a world with no light, the coldness of the deep, deep water tells you that you're entering a danger zone.

"It couldn't be..." Lulala let out a fake laugh. She was feeling a coldness like that deep-sea water throughout her entire body.

She laughed hard with Tisalia. She exchanged words with Kay and Lorna. She made small talk with Sapphee and spoke with Arahnia, who looked like she was enjoying being alone. Then she acted as a go-between for Memé and Illy, who were taking jabs at each other about something or other. This all happened in a short amount of time as she moved around the venue.

If a merfolk's body is wet, it can slither around on its belly. Lulala used that trick to move around the inn and make sure all the guests saw her. Most of Lindworm's monsters were at the celebration that night. So long as she showed her face here and there, no one would notice if she snuck out for a bit. She wasn't just an innocent singer; she was strategizing, though no one would ever suspect that from looking at her face.

Lulala was cunning, desperate to live, loved to make money, and would do anything for love. The mermaid in the fairy tale was the same way. She'd wanted legs so badly that she was willing to give up her voice.

Lulala snuck out to the Waterways, making sure the splash

as she entered the water was small that no one would notice her leaving. She headed to the fountain in the central plaza, her normal place of work.

Once she arrived, she didn't come out of the water right away. She only poked her head up furtively.

They're not here...

Many monsters have a nictitating membrane in their eyes. It is an organ that birds, reptiles, frogs, and other animals have as well. Basically, it's a translucent film that protects the eyeballs. It is also sometimes called a horizontal eyelid. Merfolk protect their eyes when they're in the water by closing this membrane. The merfolk nictitating membrane is highly advanced and, even if it is closed, allows for clear visibility.

Lulala looked around the plaza with her membranes still closed. She was nervous, afraid of getting caught for something she shouldn't be doing.

Maybe he didn't mean the plaza...

Lulala moved away from the fountain, still hidden under the water. It seemed like the doppelgänger would want to avoid places with a lot of people, and the plaza was always bustling around the fountain. Maybe Glenn and the doppelgänger were on a back street. There was a narrow alley not far from the central plaza.

I'll go check.

The Waterways were everywhere in Lindworm. But that didn't mean they were all comfortable for merfolk to travel through. The area around the central plaza was better, but, even there, the water flow was stagnant compared to the canal, and it was hard to breathe with gills. In the southern area of the town, the water flowed even less, so Lulala tried her best to avoid it. The closer she got to the back streets, the weaker the current became, which meant less oxygen in the water.

Damn...

There weren't many other merfolk in the Waterways at this time of night. There were even fewer lamps, and it was getting hard to see in the water.

Ouch!

But all her trouble was worth it. Lulala finally spotted someone in a white coat at the end of an alley. Lulala stuck her head out of the water to get a better look.

He wasn't alone.

What? Miss Kunai?

For some reason, Kunai was next to Glenn. There was no reason for her to be invited to the celebration, so it wasn't strange that she was out here. What bothered her was that Kunai had something on her back... A casket? It was big enough that it could have easily held Lulala.

Is it a date? No... No way.

The combination of Glenn and Kunai was... Well, it wasn't impossible. But the fact that she was holding a casket made it seem unlikely that they were on a date.

Then Lulala saw a familiar face behind them.

There it is!

So, Glenn *had* gone to meet Lulala's doppelgänger. She still didn't know why Kunai was there, but it looked like the three of them were talking about something. Lulala couldn't hear what they were saying from where she was.

Hey... It can *talk!*

The fake Lulala was arguing about something. It had never spoken to her down in the canal, had never let her hear its voice. Lulala wanted to hear what they were talking about, but she balked.

What am I doing?

Why was she following Glenn and peeking out of the Waterways? She'd come to express her love, but she'd never intended to take it this far. Even if they weren't on a date, whatever this was, it was none of her business.

It's nothing to do with...me.

All she'd done was give the doppelgänger food.

Glenn was probably only there to provide medical treatment for someone. She didn't want to get in the way of his job, and, most of all, she didn't want him to know that she had followed him.

If only she had legs like that doppelgänger. Would Glenn see her as a woman then? She wondered if he'd heard her singing at the inn.

Ahhh... Lulala sunk back into the water.

It was a stupid idea. If she grew legs, she wouldn't be able to sing anymore. She might be able to walk next to Glenn, but she'd lose the voice she was so proud of. If she couldn't choose Glenn over her voice, then she couldn't become the little mermaid.

That was when it happened.

The *thing* appeared.

"What?"

Just when she was about to go home. Lulala stuck her face out of the water and looked at *the thing* carefully.

What was it?

Lulala couldn't explain what she was seeing. Skadi knew a lot of things, so maybe she'd know. But Lulala had no idea how to describe the doppelgänger's true form, even though she'd seen something similar in the sea before.

To be blunt, what she saw was…a lump of flesh.

It's a blob…

That was the closest thing Lulala could think of.

Having lived in the sea, she knew that massive chunks of flesh were sometimes cast ashore. They looked frightening. Land dwellers called them blobs or globsters, but they were nothing to be repulsed by. The original forms of these blobs were usually rotten whale or orca carcasses washed ashore by the waves. For some reason, though, they didn't look like whales to humans.

But it went without saying that carcasses didn't move.

This lump of flesh moved, however.

It's…alive?

It was a frightening sight. The lump of flesh had something that looked like horns, and it was making writhing motions. Its flat appearance made it look like a sea slug moving across the ocean floor, but its red and black surface made it look like a corpse whose skin was peeling off. The bottom of it was full of gaps which looked like mouths. Lulala wondered if the chunk of flesh had a real mouth as well. A big one. She imagined it opening that mouth wide.

She decided to call it a blob, for the time being.

Glenn, Kunai, and the fake Lulala didn't seem surprised at the appearance of the blob at all.

"There it is!"

Lulala heard Kunai's voice.

Kunai threw down the casket and stood in front the others, confronting the blob. As bodyguard to the Draconess, she showed no fear facing the unknown chunk of flesh. Kunai balled her fist, looking straight at it with her keen eyes.

The blob opened its mouth wide, making a glub-sound.

I was right, thought Lulala.

The chunk of flesh looked just like a frog when it opened its mouth. What was Kunai going to do? Her specialty—boxing—wouldn't do anything against a blob.

It would be better to try defeating them with a water gun. Just as Lulala thought that—

GULP.

"Aaaaghhh?!"

Kunai was swallowed whole by the blob's giant mouth.

"Noooooo!" Lulala immediately realized her folly in letting her voice be heard.

Glenn turned around when he heard her scream. Now he would definitely figure out that she'd been following him.

"Lulala?! What are you doing here?"

"Oh. Uh! Don't worry about me! What about Miss Kunai?!"

"Oh, she's fine."

"Whaaaat?!" Lulala screamed again, frustrated by Glenn's lack of interest.

But Glenn was calmly observing the blob. Having swallowed Kunai whole from her head to her feet, the blob was now acting strange. It wriggled and squirmed, as if it were in pain. Something poked out of its body, but not like a tentacle or a horn; something else. The blob no longer looked like it was rearing up to attack.

"Does it seem like it's...in pain?"

"Doppelgänger, is this right?"

Even though their faces were identical, Glenn seemed to be able to distinguish between the doppelgänger and Lulala. He didn't think in the slightest that Lulala had grown legs. When Lulala thought about it, it seemed obvious. She was glad. She wasn't the mermaid from the fairy tale; she wouldn't grow legs.

But that was fine. She felt like Glenn was telling her that she was a mermaid, so it was only natural that she had a mermaid's body and lived in the Waterways. Even if it were only her own assumption, she felt it was proof that Glenn saw Lulala as a mermaid.

It may have been her imagination, but Lulala thought she saw a streak of light appear in the blob's body.

"Oof."

The blob's body tore from the inside. The amorphous flesh split, and Kunai appeared with a dagger in her hand.

"It'll be a cold day in hell before I let you eat me!"

After being swallowed, she'd made her escape from inside the body with a dagger. Kunai's martial arts skills were so advanced that she could do things Lulala never would have dreamed of. She'd easily bisected this unknown *thing*.

Kunai jumped out of the blob's body. She rolled down the alley and landed on one knee. She was covered in some sort of sticky slime, but unharmed.

"I'm sure I wouldn't taste good anyway," she said, in a self-deprecating way.

After being sliced through with a dagger, the blob was limp. It didn't show any signs of movement. It seemed like Kunai had exterminated it by pretending to let herself be eaten.

But it was all a mystery.

What was the relationship between Glenn and the doppelgänger? What was the blob that had suddenly appeared and eaten Kunai? Lulala wanted to ask Glenn to explain, but he was staring at the blob intently.

"Dr. Glenn, thank you for your help."

Kunai looked down into the waterway. Her keen eyes stopped on Lulala's face.

"Lulala! Behind you!"

"Huh?" Lulala felt something slippery. She turned around.

Behind her, in the waterway, was another blob with its mouth wide open. It was about to swallow her.

"Aggh!"

Lulala moved quickly. She used her tail to slap the surface of the water with all her might. On the rebound, she jumped out of the water. Her landing didn't go well, and she ended up smacking the ground with her stomach, but she gained some ground. Then she used her slimy body to slip away.

But—

Agh... It's too fast...

The blob jumped out of the water and thrust itself at Lulala with its mouth wide open. The one that had swallowed Kunai was nothing compared to the speed of this one.

Ahh.

Lulala now realized that the last one must have already been in a weakened state. When she thought about it now, these blobs were like a cross between a sea slug and a frog, adapted to the water. The one that had been in the water until only a moment ago had strength to spare. It wriggled forward quickly, aiming for Lulala.

Agh!

Lulala closed her eyes without thinking. She was sure she tasted better than Kunai, a corpse. She had been chased by a shark in the sea before, but this blob was far more massive than the shark had been...and it was quick. She couldn't run away.

Somebody called her name; it was either Glenn or Kunai. Maybe it was both of them. Lulala had closed her eyes in fear of being eaten, so she didn't know who was calling out to her.

"Lulala!"

Who was it that called her now?

She heard her name a third time. Something hit her and sent her flying. That's when she opened her eyes. In front of her was a face identical to hers.

Lulala had protected Lulala.

"Oh..."

It couldn't speak. It was like the fairy tale, as if its voice had been stolen. She wanted to call the doppelgänger by its name, but Lulala didn't know what the *girl* with her face was called.

GULP.

At that moment, the other Lulala who had protected her was swallowed whole by the blob.

× × ✖ × ×

Glenn Litbeit had some regrets.

He hadn't realized that Lulala was in the alley, and that was why Lulala had been put in danger.

"Doctor... Doctor!"

"It's okay. You're okay, Lulala."

"It's not okay. I-I was eaten!" Lulala must have been confused. She was crying and yelling.

That doppelgänger did have the same face as Lulala. If they'd had any sort of exchange in the canal, then it would make sense that they had the same face. Glenn held Lulala, calming her down as he checked the situation.

The chunk of flesh that had first appeared was still, same as when it had thrown up Kunai. It was exactly how the doppelgänger with Lulala's face had described it. It looked horrifying, but it had lost all its will to act. Sure, it had mistakenly eaten Kunai, but now it had gone limp. The other chunk of flesh, which had eaten the Lulala doppelgänger, was soaking wet but silent. It didn't seem like it had lost its strength, nor did he think it would stop moving just because it ate the doppelgänger.

"Umm, Doctor... What should I..."

"Listen to me, Lulala. This is very important, so I need to you listen closely. The doppelgänger was your friend, right?"

"Friend—yes. Yes, it was! I'm sure we were friends..." Lulala had had her doubts until she saw it with her own eyes.

"In that case you don't need to worry. Those are all doppelgängers."

"Huh?" Lulala's eyes widened.

It wasn't something even Glenn could fully understand.

"Let me explain." Kunai moved to a spot where she could shield Glenn and Lulala. Her movements were that of an experienced bodyguard. Lulala couldn't have asked for more.

Kunai continued speaking without taking her eyes off the chunk of flesh. "The Lindworm patrol team was concerned about the rumors around town, so they have been tracking the doppelgänger for some time now. They couldn't catch it, but then Dr. Cthulhy shared her opinion with the Draconess that the doppelgänger was traveling through the Waterways. The patrol team took extreme care and was finally able to track down the doppelgänger, but—"

"Th-they didn't catch it?"

"The opposite. They caught too many."

"What? What?"

Glenn had, of course, been dumbfounded when he heard

this report too. The shapeless chunks of flesh—the true form of the doppelgängers—had been found in the Waterways. Many of them.

"Within a few days of searching, they found ten creatures that looked like those chunks of flesh. Each one was about the size of a piglet, and they were all slow-witted. It was easy to catch them."

"Oh..."

"But once they were caught, the problem was keeping them. At first, they were put in sealed bins, but the doppelgängers were able to open them from the inside. They ran away immediately. Then, they were kept in a locked room, but they stretched through the cracks and unlocked the door. It was really quite the problem."

That had been the case with the heart at the hospital as well.

These doppelgängers couldn't be contained. Someone had come up with the idea to collect them all in one place and burn them, but the Draconess wouldn't allow it. She wouldn't stand for the death penalty when no crime had been committed.

"Th-then what happened?"

"Dione from the harpy village gave us the biggest hint."

"The...Giant Goddess? Illy visits her often."

"That's right. The Giant Goddess wrote us a letter."

Dione had written a letter to Glenn.

The letter said that the doppelgänger was, in fact, an ancient being called a shoggoth. It was especially adept at dividing itself into pieces. As well—

"It seems the doppelgänger has a nucleus that can instruct all of the pieces."

"A...nucleus?"

"The doppelgänger was able to collect various, disparate pieces of information to circumvent the arena guards and the patrol team. That would be impossible for just one monster. Dione figured out that not only could it collect this information, as easily as fairies can, it could also integrate that information and give appropriate instructions based on it. The doppelgänger was actually a group of many individuals."

"A...group?" Lulala had nothing but questions for what Glenn was saying.

"So we've been searching for the piece giving the instructions, directing the divided parts—the nucleus. We figured we could reason with it."

"Th-this is confusing..."

Squish.

The chunk of flesh that had eaten the fake Lulala moved. No—the fake Lulala must have instructed it to move—and to eat it. If Lulala understood everything she had been told so far, that fake Lulala was the nucleus Glenn and the others had been searching for.

"Lulala, the doppelgänger that you met was the nucleus."

"Wh-what? What?" Lulala still didn't quite understand.

The chunk of flesh wriggled and stacked itself on top of the other chunk of flesh, the one that had failed to eat Kunai. *So, these chunks of flesh were being directed by the fake Lulala, and that's why they gathered here.* The doppelgänger scraps that had scattered throughout Lindworm were now becoming one.

"The celebration was a front for the plan to bring the doppelgängers together. We figured that if everyone was at the celebration, then no one would be in this alley."

"S-sorry..." Lulala apologized, feeling as if she were being blamed.

"No, that was my fault. I don't know what the patrol is doing. I told them to keep watch so that no one would come in..." Kunai shook her head. She had a gentle smile on her face. If Lulala had snuck through the Waterways, then the patrol team wouldn't have noticed her.

Glenn was watching the chunks of flesh that had just become one. They were no longer the hideous red and black forms that they had been only moments ago. They had turned into a translucent slime-like form, as if the chunks were more controlled as a single unit.

But that thought only lasted a moment. The gel-like body converged, and the doppelgänger changed forms again. The process resembled a slime's transformation. Now, the previous chunks of flesh were out of the nucleus's control, probably because they'd been separated from it for so long.

"Doppelgänger, can you hear me?" Glenn didn't know if this was the correct way to address it.

But the small form, which now looked like Skadi, nodded.

"You took on the form of Skadi and infested her body. When you were cut out of her, you needed a new food source. Were you searching for a new host?"

The doppelgänger nodded again.

The objective of all parasites was clearly to use the nutrients of their hosts. This doppelgänger had become Skadi's heart and altered her veins, taking in her blood. Dragon blood was a precious alchemical material and had no equivalent. It must have been a valuable source of nutrients as well.

But Glenn had removed the doppelgänger from Skadi's body.

"Have you already found a new host? After separating into pieces and circulating Lindworm, did you find a suitable place?"

This time, the doppelgänger shook its head. It hadn't.

The doppelgänger had an extremely high aptitude for learning. It knew well why it had failed at infesting Skadi's body—it had affected the body of its host. Plus, there was a doctor in this town. Infesting someone else just meant it would be removed again. To figure out how to live without being a parasite or wanting for nutrients, it had taken on the form of people in the town so that it could observe other living beings.

"I am a doctor. And you are having trouble living. In other words, you are not in a healthy state, and I want to help you."

"..."

"Skadi said she will forgive you. She is still recovering, and she doesn't plan to hold a grudge. But if you are going to cause harm to the residents, you can't stay in this town." Glenn's face was stern.

While it wasn't a problem that the doppelgänger had divided and spread throughout the city, it *was* a problem that each of the individual parts had begun acting on their own. The chunks of flesh weren't trying to infest people as parasites; they were trying to obtain nutrients, as predators. The possibility of residents being attacked made Glenn anxious.

In the letter from Dione, she said that if the doppelgänger lacked nourishment, there was a possibility it would cause direct harm by becoming predatory. When that happened, the piece would no longer listen to the directions of the nucleus and would continue hunting.

Lulala had narrowly escaped being eaten.

But before that could happen, the doppelgänger had bravely shielded Lulala. The doppelgänger was unlike other living creatures, but that didn't mean it was incompatible with them. It did not view life lightly. Glenn believed that meant he could reason with it.

"Lulala, as its friend, you understand, right?"

With the help of the patrol team, they'd found the nucleus hidden in the Waterways. When Kunai heard the report, she was surprised. She didn't understand why the nucleus looked exactly like Lulala but didn't have the lower body of a mermaid.

The nucleus hadn't become predatory because Lulala had been sneaking it food. Therefore, the nucleus hadn't lost the original intent of the doppelgänger and was trying to figure out a way to become one again with all of its divided parts. This was in line with Skadi's desire to immobilize the doppelgänger.

"The Draconess has a proposal." Kunai, who had been standing by listening, pulled over the coffin. "Doppelgänger, if you plan to live in the town...she will prepare an appropriate occupation for you in the district on the north side. The duties of the job are probably too easy for you."

"..."

"The conditions of the deal are that you are not allowed to attack anyone ever again. What is your answer?"

The doppelgänger was silent.

The coffin Kunai had prepared held a skeleton. Skadi had come up with the whole idea. She thought the doppelgänger might be able to become the face the town needed with these bones. In other words, by borrowing the face of someone who was no longer part of this world. That way, the doppelgänger would no longer take on the image of others.

The bones in the coffin belonged to a skeleton that had already passed—the former manager of the graveyard city. Skadi was proposing that the doppelgänger occupy the skeleton and become the manager.

The doppelgänger looked at Lulala and nodded. "I...accept assignment."

The doppelgänger shifted its body. It turned into its slime form and pressed its jiggling body into the coffin. In a moment, the coffin was filled to the brim with a semi-transparent gel-like substance. It wasn't long before the skeleton began to change. A protean substance was attached to the manager's bones, and that flesh started to take form.

The doppelgänger had never met the previous manager, but it seemed to be reproducing its living form based on the shape of the bones. More and more flesh covered the skeleton. At the very least, the face and the hair were a reproduction of what the skeleton might have looked like in life. The body was still semi-transparent, and the skeleton inside showed through. Something like small air bubbles dotted its torso.

The face was pale, the goggling eyes striking—a defining characteristic of this new being. It was strikingly beautiful, and seemed cold, but those eyes gave it a certain charm.

"Acquiring body information from bones. Reproducibility, 47%. No impediments. Glenn Litbeit. Lulala Heine. Kunai Zenow. Acknowledged. Commence activity. Am I conversing?"

"Y-yes it seems fine."

"No impediments in conversation ability, communication." The doppelgänger stood up.

It was completely naked, but it just looked like gelatin stuck to bones. There was nothing suggestive about its appearance. Its method of talking was stiff, but that seemed to be the nature of the doppelgänger's thoughts.

"Permission requested to ask a question."

"Uhh... You don't have to be so obedient. We are residents of the same town."

"Understood. No obedience. Glenn Litbeit categorized as 'town resident.'" The response was still stiff. The doppelgänger looked straight at Glenn with its goggling eyes. "We are currently acting in the interest of nutrient supply. We have no objection to executing the new duties, but if there is no nutrient supply, activities will cease or...a shift to predatory state is possible."

"You will be paid a salary, and you can also send for fresh foods from the Aluloona Plantation." Kunai answered the doppelgänger's question.

The doppelgänger let out a breath of either disgust or exhaustion, Glenn didn't know which. It was hard to read the cold expression in its big eyes.

"Understood. We will execute duties under those conditions. That was all we were looking for when we divided. A new nutrient supply..."

"What kind of food do you like?"

"Beef." It answered right away. Considering it essentially preyed on other living things, this seemed like a natural request. "Acquired body for activity and means of nutrient supply. Will now execute duties as manager of graveyard city. Lulala Heine."

"Huh? Oh, yes?"

The doppelgänger had called on Lulala without changing its facial expression. She hadn't been expecting it to speak to her. She was having enough trouble following all of this.

"Thank you." The doppelgänger smiled. Its face was supposed to have changed to someone else's, but in that moment, the smile looked just like Lulala.

Lulala was dumbstruck.

Just when she'd thought that the doppelgänger with her face had been eaten by a blob, it recovered and used the bones of someone it didn't know to become human. Lulala had heard of the graveyard city, but she hadn't realized that the manager was gone. And now the doppelgänger was the new manager?

She couldn't keep up.

"Thanks to Lulala Heine's aid, we were supplied with nutrients.

That made it easy to maintain the nucleus, and we were able to propose a solution to Glenn Litbeit and Kunai Zenow. We will be able to return to a single existence."

"Ah, y-yes?"

"Also, of the many imitations, the Lulala Heine imitation provided the greatest opportunity for learning. We collected information about language and emotion, and details about the human relationships and social order in the town."

"I-I don't understand what you're saying."

The words the doppelgänger was using were too difficult for Lulala, who had never attended school. But she did understand that she was being thanked many times over. All she had done was treat the doppelgänger as a friend, but it seemed that that had been good for it. She'd never thought that simply bringing it food and speaking to it would lead to this.

"In that case, we will use a means of communication other than language." The doppelgänger held out its hand.

The hand was covered with a semi-transparent purple substance, and bones were visible through it. But the doppelgänger's bones weren't eroded like the corpses Lulala had seen in the ocean. The skeleton must have been skillfully embalmed.

Lulala knew what it meant when a hand was extended, so she grabbed the doppelgänger's hand. It felt a bit slimy, but that wasn't a problem for Lulala, who lived in the water.

"Lulala, what did you tell it?"

"Oh, uh well..."

"That is a confidential matter. Set to maximum security level.

In local slang terms, 'girl talk.'" The doppelgänger used difficult words, but it was still understandable.

Perhaps it really is a mischievous being, thought Lulala. It was hard to tell from the lack of facial expression, but its words seemed humorous.

"Oh, Doctor, the celebration..."

"Oh... That's right. I wonder if Sapphee is mad. I haven't greeted Miss Tisalia yet, even though she invited me..."

Lulala remembered why she was there.

When she thought about it, she'd gotten caught up in this mess because she went searching for Glenn after noticing he wasn't at the celebration. It would have been the perfect opportunity to see him...but he had this all planned out.

She'd almost been eaten by a blob.

That was right. It was all Glenn's fault.

Lulala was on land now, and Glenn just happened to be holding on to her, supporting her upper body. If she'd grown legs, there would be no need for him to do so. She decided to stay put for a bit and enjoy the moment, even though she could never tell Sapphee about it.

"Let's sing a song." The doppelgänger abruptly spoke. "A song Lulala Heine sang many times."

"Huh?"

"We speak with a great deal of difficulty. We have determined that it is challenging to correctly express gratitude. Songs rapidly improve the rate of conveying feelings."

"Oh, ummm..." She didn't really understand.

Before Lulala could stop it, the doppelgänger began singing.

"—————————♪"

It was a requiem.

The voice was exactly like Lulala's. So, it wasn't just appearances that it could mimic, it could also imitate voices. The vibrato, trills, and breathing were all precisely the same as Lulala.

The doppelgänger wasn't singing. It was simply reproducing Lulala's singing voice. But the sound was still full of emotion.

"..."

It was just like the doppelgänger had said. Even though its voice was really *her* voice, its feelings were conveyed clearly.

Lulala tightened her hold on Glenn. He would probably stay by her side for as long as she was on land.

I wonder if it's okay.

She glanced at Glenn, wondering if her feelings of love would be conveyed to him through the doppelgänger's song, even though that was an impossibility. Someday, when she grew up—when she was Sapphee's age—Lulala thought she might have the courage to tell Glenn how she felt. Even if she never grew legs, she would always have her voice. And if she became a charming mermaid, then maybe she could charm him.

For now, she would keep her feelings hidden in the water.

Lulala chuckled to herself, mischievously imagining Glenn's face when she would tell him about her feelings. She was looking forward to it.

Full of emotion, Lulala joined the doppelgänger in singing.

The two voices rang through the night.

Lulala felt as if meeting the girl with the same face as her had made her life as a mermaid more fun, as if she had been given courage...and a secret.

She was so, so very happy.

EPILOGUE:
The Doppelgänger of Graveyard City

GLENN IMMEDIATELY wrote a reply to Dione.

In his letter, he mentioned the fake heart, the shoggoth/doppelgänger and the fact that she—yes, she—was now the manager of the graveyard city. He gave Dione a detailed account of her many faces and forms, and how she became a member of the town.

They'd been able to find the fake Lulala—the nucleus—all thanks to Dione's letter. Dione was the one who'd given them the details of shoggoth biology. Glenn thought the kind-hearted Giant Goddess would be glad to learn that the doppelgänger had been assigned to manage the graveyard city, and that she'd been given a form appropriate to the role.

He also wrote about the celebration.

After the incident, Sapphee had, of course, interrogated him. He'd also ended up listening to Tisalia ramble on about her match. Lulala seemed to be in high spirits. She sang many more songs once they'd returned to the party.

Dione would probably have wanted to come. But she would also probably say that it was enough for her just to read Glenn's letter. Glenn wanted to visit her and see how she was doing, but without wings, the peak of the Vivre Mountains was a bit too far away. At least corresponding by letter would make Dione smile.

"Doctor, are you ready?"

Just as he finished writing the letter, he heard Sapphee's voice, as if she had timed it that way on purpose.

"Yeah, I'm coming."

"Okay."

He'd leave visiting Dione to people who could easily make it up the mountain. Glenn had enough on his plate simply taking care of those he *was* able to visit. The Vivre Mountains may be too far, but he could at least make it to the outskirts of Lindworm.

Well.

It was hard to tell what the true face of the person he was going to see that day might be.

"Well, I never."

A few days had passed since Tisalia's celebration. Glenn was on his way to Deadlich Graveyard City with Sapphee. The road up the hill that led to the graveyard city was somber as always.

They were going to the graveyard city because the new manager, the doppelgänger, had invited them. Apparently, she'd heard that Glenn was a doctor.

"I think the manager should have come to the city," complained Sapphee, holding a parasol as she walked.

"I'm sure it's awkward for her. She caused quite a fuss. Her divided parts really behaved violently. A lot happened."

"Yes, it does seem that *a lot happened*, Dr. Glenn. Of course, I only heard about everything after the fact."

Sapphee's words stung. She was still mad that he had kept her out of the loop during the ordeal.

"I said I was sorry. The doppelgänger was causing nothing but problems, and I knew it was going to be dangerous, so I couldn't get you involved. I discussed it with Kunai beforehand."

"I'm not saying you should have taken me with you. But if I'd known what was going on, then I could have instructed Lulala better at the celebration. She went looking for you."

"Hmm..." That had definitely been Glenn's biggest mistake in this ordeal.

He'd put Lulala in danger. In the end, she was unscathed, but that was only because the doppelgänger had shielded her from the part of it that had become violent. Glenn deeply regretted letting Lulala get involved.

"If I hadn't complained to Lulala about how you were gone..."

"No, that's not right, Sapphee."

"I'd been drinking..." If there was alcohol available, then Sapphee would drink, but that wasn't the issue.

Glenn was at a loss for what to say to her.

His own thoughtlessness had made even Sapphee, whom he hadn't wanted to involve, feel bad. It was easy to tell Sapphee that it wasn't her fault, but would she accept that fact with just his words?

"Saphentite Neikes, I declare that you were 0% at fault for what transpired."

They heard a mechanical-sounding voice.

"99% of the fault in this issue lies with us, the parties involved. The attempted predation of Lulala Heine was also our doing. The biggest factor was that we were unable to control ourselves as a unified being. Therefore, the fault of Saphentite Neikes is nil."

"You..." When had the doppelgänger shown up?

It seemed they'd reached the graveyard city. They hadn't been paying attention while they were walking, then suddenly, they came upon her, the doppelgänger, polishing the gate to the entrance and speaking to Sapphee so matter-of-factly. Though, perhaps she was also saying that the whole ordeal was 1% Glenn's fault.

The doppelgänger stared at them with her goggling eyes.

"N-nice to meet you, Miss Doppelgänger. I am Saphentite..."

"Verification, recognition complete. Information matches data from time of doppelgänger activities. Previously, I was only observing you, but now that we are conversing, I place Saphentite Neikes in the category of 'town resident.' Nice to meet you."

"Wh-what...?" Sapphee cocked her head to one side.

It was a bit strange. Her words were extremely unique and hard to understand. Sapphee thought the doppelgänger might behave according to a different logic than humans or monsters. There were even parts of what she said that Glenn didn't understand. But Sapphee could at least understand that the doppelgänger was telling her not to fret.

"I will also provide important supplemental information."

"Huh?"

"We have acquired a new name as town resident. We borrowed the previous manager's name. Our name is Second-Generation Molly Vanitas. Approved by City Council. This is our official name in Lindworm. Utmost importance, requires recognition."

"O-okay… I understand. Miss Molly. Nice to meet you again."

"Dr. Glenn. Dr. Saphentite. Thank you for coming to the graveyard city." The doppelgänger—no, Molly—held out her hand.

The hand had five gelatin-like fingers, but the bones were still visible, as if she hadn't finished her imitation. But Sapphee grabbed the hand without reserve.

The goggling eyes seemed to smile, just a little.

Molly Vanitas.

As far as Glenn could tell, she had changed. She looked more complete than when she'd first attached herself to the skeleton and reproduced its body. The biggest change was that she was now wearing a monk's robe, though the fabric was part of Molly's flesh. Around her chest, abdomen, and waist, the robe had blended with Molly's gelatin body tissue, making it look like there were holes in her clothing.

From Glenn's observations, there were only two pieces of Molly that weren't part of her flesh. First was the band she wore on her upper arm. She'd gotten it for her role on the Lindworm City Council. Kunai wore the same kind of band when she served as a guard in the Waterways, while Molly's arm band bore the seal of the manager of the graveyard city. The City Council had probably presented it to her in recognition of her succeeding the former manager.

The second item was the shovel she held in her right hand. It had clearly been used for many years, and it was no ordinary shovel. If you looked closely, you could see that the tip was sharp, and the blade had been tempered to resemble the end of a spear—something only a swordsmith would have the skills to forge. It was more like a weapon that also happened to serve as a shovel.

"I don't remember you having that shovel before."

"It belonged to the previous manager. They say she used it to punish ghosts who didn't follow orders. It has been consecrated to use on spirits. I plan to utilize it as well."

"O-oh." It seemed the graveyard city manager had to be somewhat adept in martial arts.

"I haven't really been to the graveyard city. Is it lively?"

"Well... Yes." Glenn vaguely nodded in response to Sapphee.

This was Glenn's second visit to Deadlich Graveyard City, but it had changed since the first. It was still as dark as night, even in the daytime. But the ruins had been cleaned, the ivy and moss had been removed, and the dirt had been wiped away. There was no unpleasant feeling of something lurking, trying to possess visitors.

And throughout the ruins, zombies were installing several lanterns. These were made from hollowed-out radishes and pumpkins, and they brightened up the atmosphere significantly.

"Why lanterns?"

"To revamp the graveyard city's image. As the second-generation manager, I plan to fix our frightening reputation. If there are jobs available, if we can make this place a friendly part of Lindworm, then it won't get out of control again. Everyone wants Deadlich to be a nice place to live. The first task is to address the low level of light."

"It seems like it would be hard to manage so many lights."

Lamps meant candles. Even with so many zombies and skeletons pitching in, it would still take a lot of work to light each and every one.

"No problem. The lamps are empty inside. No candles."

"What?"

"We're still testing it, but we've established a candle-less light source. We will request opinions for further development. Operation Will o' the Wisp!"

With a series of popping sounds, the numerous lamps lining the ruins lit up, one after another the instant Molly gave the command. They also illuminated the path where Glenn was standing. The light was weaker than that of candles, but the orange glow that lit the gloomy graveyard city nevertheless had a warmth to it. Collectively, the lights were even brighter than that of a parade.

"This..."

"We've increased the amount of light in the graveyard city by 80% using will o' the wisps created by ghosts. We hope to change the image of the district and create a unique attraction. We anticipate improved rate of customer interest, tourist income, and perceived image. The concept is 'a bright and fun haunted house.'"

"Hahaha."

"Furthermore, the light is not natural, so it is the perfect solution for vampires and other species who can't handle sunlight. As of now, there are zero residents objecting to this plan." Molly's expression never changed in the slightest.

Looking at the lit-up sign in front of him—which read *Deadlich Hotel*—Glenn had to admit it was a pretty good strategy. The evidence of this was Sapphee, a true romantic, speechlessly gazing at the illumination. Using light from will o' the wisps was an unusual idea, but one of the advantages was that all of the lamps could be lit at once.

"Add correction to expected village value. Also consider further appeal to couples and honeymoons."

"M-Miss Molly!"

"Saphentite has the heart of a young girl. She loves this sort of thing. The information I acquired from Lulala was correct. I am grateful for the provision of such valuable information."

"Hey! Stop it! That's not why we came here today!" Sapphee was angry at Molly's lack of reserve.

Glenn was more than merely moved. When he'd visited with Kunai, it had looked like the residents of the graveyard city had no cohesion or unity. But maybe that wasn't the case. Now, the undead were making efforts to decorate, and the ghosts were providing perfectly coordinated light.

This was all thanks to the skill of Second-Generation Molly Vanitas.

Only a few days had passed since the new manager was appointed, but it was as if a veteran general was commanding the entire graveyard city.

"It's amazing that the ghosts are obeying so well."

"The biggest reason they ran amuck was boredom. They just needed a clear policy and an occupation. Ghosts, phantoms, zombies, skeletons—everyone likes commotion. If there's a lively festival every night, they don't even consider going outside the fence."

The lamps all went out at once. Only the ones around Glenn, Sapphee, and Molly remained lit. That was plenty of light, and they had no trouble walking.

"The lights went out?"

"Operation Will o' the Wisp requires general mobilization of the ghosts, so it only runs for a few minutes. From here on, normal light is used."

The flashy performance was probably reserved mainly for tourists.

Molly led them into the graveyard city. As Glenn and Sapphee followed her, the lamps behind them went out and the ones ahead lit up. The ghosts were probably turning them on and off. Glenn was grateful for the guide lights in the dark graveyard city.

"We've arrived."

Molly had led them to the church. She held the door open, and all three of them went inside.

"Okay then..." Glenn nodded to Sapphee.

They hadn't come to the graveyard city to see its new source of illumination, though they were pleasantly surprised, of course, by the lights created by the endless ghost lamps.

"I will begin the health exam now."

"Affirmative. I entrust Dr. Glenn with checking my vitals." Second-Generation Molly Vanitas nodded her head deeply.

Today's task was to check the status of Molly's transformed flesh and whether there were any health concerns. Glenn was a bit nervous, as he would have to report the results to the City Council.

"I will start by declaring if there are any abnormalities in the various functions."

He wasn't completely convinced that a health examination was necessary for a living being that defied all common sense.

× × ✖ × ×

Glenn began by observing Molly's monk robe.

There were several holes in it, mainly on the right side. Not just holes—Molly probably had insufficient constitutive substance, so she was unable to reproduce clothing in those places. A semi-transparent purple gel filled the space under her clothes. The previous manager's skeleton was visible inside the substance.

While there was some gel in the chest area, the surfaces of a few of Molly's ribs were exposed—specifically the eighth through tenth ribs on the left side—as if she didn't have enough body tissue there, either.

Glenn moved on to her face and head. It looked like each strand of hair had been meticulously reproduced. The hood of her robe had probably been similarly reproduced from her flesh.

"Hmm. Excuse me."

"Mm."

Glenn touched one of the exposed ribs. Given how old the skeleton was, he wanted to make sure it wouldn't deteriorate. However, the rib felt slimy, as if the surface was coated with gel as well.

"Argh!"

"I'm sorry! Did that hurt?"

"No problem. I am capable of controlling my sense of pain."

It's not really a problem, but...

Glenn couldn't overlook the fact that Molly had winced, just for a moment, and her face had gone as slack as slime. Her hood had also changed form, losing its color, and she'd grown something like horns. Perhaps she was unable to keep her form when she was taken off-guard.

However, it was only for a moment. Her hood and eyeballs went right back to how they'd been before. There were also popping noises, as if the reaction had created air bubbles in the gel.

Glenn looked up and saw that Sapphee was arranging items in the corner of the room. She'd brought a stock of preservatives and deodorants that Molly had requested for the zombies who needed them.

He looked at Molly's face. Other than how pale it was, it looked the same as a human's.

"Almost everything looks pretty good."

"I dislike this vague expression. What is 'almost'? If 70% is good, then 30% is not?"

"Umm..." Glenn wasn't ready to be questioned like that. He wasn't sure how to answer with those big goggling eyes staring at him, unmoving. "As a doctor, I see no problems. You are 100% healthy. But...I have some questions."

"Dr. Glenn is here as mandated by the City Council. You are permitted to ask questions."

"Are you experiencing any inconveniences in your life? What I mean is, do you have any problems living in a town? You were previously living somewhere else...right?"

"Intent of question is unclear. More details."

"I'm concerned that you feel trapped here."

There were no problems with Molly's body. Actually, he thought Molly probably knew more about the state of her body than he did. It looked like she had the ability to analyze as well as repair herself. She may be different from other living beings, but there didn't seem to be any abnormalities. Glenn was more concerned with her emotional adaptability.

"Infestation of Skadi Dragenfelt was for the purpose of acquiring nutrients only. However, there was no consideration for the body of the host. It was an immature way to live. We have learned. The optimum way to acquire nutrients is to live as a town member and fulfill duties. Incorrect?"

"I think that's correct."

"So long as we can fulfill the role of manager and earn compensation, we are Molly Vanitas, manager of the graveyard city." The doppelgänger spoke these words without any eye movement.

Glenn had no response to this. Even though Molly had only been appointed days earlier, she'd already shown tremendous results in restructuring the graveyard city.

"Originally, we served an existence higher than us. The state of working under the order of a dragon fulfills the purpose of our creation."

"Were you created by someone?"

"Details are unclear. Due to a long dormant state, that information is lost. It is possible to search for a relationship to the scylla species."

"No, that won't be necessary."

It seemed Molly didn't even know herself.

Perhaps it was the ancient species called the malevolent gods, ancestors of the Scylla, who had used Molly, but the only one who knew about that was Dione. There was no reason to force Molly to recall the past when she was alive now.

"Oh, one more thing. Your bones are exposed in one area. I think it would be better to cover them entirely."

"Body tissue gross volume is currently insufficient. Chromocytes are also insufficient, so body and clothing mimicry are incomplete. This result is the most natural mimicry possible."

"Gross volume...is insufficient?"

"Some pieces that ran away after division are still unaccounted for. I am currently performing search, collection, and assimilation duties parallel to manager duties. Even after collection, there is a possibility of lost or damaged cells when diverted to mimic use. Complete mimicry will take time. It is possible to calculate an estimate, but results may be inaccurate due to insufficient information."

"What if you reduce the amount used in your chest?" Glenn asked as he looked at her bust.

Molly's chest was obviously large. Excessively. With her intellectual way of thinking, she must have already noticed.

"That would render building a relationship with Glenn Litbeit impossible."

"Excuse me?" Glenn was dumbfounded at Molly's matter-of-factness.

"After observing the everyday lives of the residents of Lindworm, we have confirmed that most female monsters have an intimate relationship with Dr. Glenn. We have analyzed that friendly relations with Dr. Glenn are beneficial to a pleasant life in this town."

"Wh-what?"

"Also, there is an apparent increase in excitement and heart-rate when Dr. Glenn is near the breasts of women. To maintain future friendship with Dr. Glenn, feminine physique with abundant flesh is essential." Molly's face was expressionless as she spoke, but she was basically saying that Dr. Glenn was only excited by looking at breasts.

Could Molly measure heartrate just by looking at someone? If so, and if it were accurate, then that was an extraordinary ability. Glenn wanted to put it to use at the clinic.

"D-Doctor! What is this all about?!" Until now, Sapphee had been unconcerned with the exam, but, for some reason, she was suddenly irate. "You're drooling over Miss Molly's chest?!"

"N-no. Wait a second. We've gotten off-topic. That's not true. Molly, you've misunderstood." Glenn was flustered and spoke without thinking. He got the feeling Molly's goggling eyes were gleaming.

"Misunderstood? That means my analysis is mistaken?"

"Uh."

"Understood. We will verify accuracy of analysis."

Had Glenn angered her? It had seemed like Molly possessed almost no emotions, but—

She suddenly opened her robe, exposing her chest.

"Ah?!"

The monk robe wasn't even made to be opened in the front. But if you considered that the robe was part of Molly, it was probably easy to change the composition of it in an instant. From the exposed chest, Glenn could see Molly's purple, semi-transparent, unique cleavage very well. The ribs were also faintly visible. He could see everything from her sternum, episternum, and costicartilage to her xiphoid. It wasn't just a normal naked body. Glenn's eyes were drawn to both its anatomical and sexual appeal.

"Increased heartrate. Slight increase in body temperature. Perspiration confirmed. Results of analysis: slight state of excitement."

"You took off your clothes to confirm that?"

"Er... This..."

Molly didn't seem to be listening at all. When he tried looking away, she reached out and grabbed Glenn's face. She was frighteningly strong. It was hard to believe she was nothing but bones and gelatin. She forced Glenn to look at her chest, seemingly unwilling to let him look away.

"I have increased transparency so it is easier to observe the bones. This has increased Dr. Glenn's excitement, which means that excitement increases when non-human elements are present in the woman."

"What did you say? Miss Molly, I need more details!" Sapphee latched onto this information.

"I hypothesize that monster women have an advantage in increasing friendliness with Dr. Glenn. Sapphee, what is your opinion of this hypothesis?"

"Yes! Yes! I think it is a very good hypothesis."

The two women spoke enthusiastically. Glenn couldn't get a word in.

"Does Dr. Glenn like lamia the best?!" Sapphee asked.

"Information is insufficient to analyze Dr. Glenn's inclinations."

"I see. Miss Molly, please make sure you collect all necessary data regarding this issue."

"Understood. Add task 'Dr. Glenn's preferred monster inclinations' to duties as new project."

Glenn was at his wit's end listening to Molly play dumb with such a straight face. Why did anyone have to analyze his inclinations? He looked for an opportunity to jump in.

"Hey, Sapphee, I think that's enough..."

"What do you mean, Doctor? This is an important topic. Do you know how much I worry because you have your hands full with so many different monster women? If you would just tell me you like lamia best, then we wouldn't have to discuss it anymore."

"I like lamia... I like all monsters!" Glenn only meant to protest, but Sapphee came back with words that stung hundreds of times over.

"You pervert! You're just a failure who can't find a human wife!"

If he said anything else, she might wrap the snake half of her body around him and constrict him.

With all the commotion in the church, the nearby lanterns flickered as if joining in. Maybe ghosts liked this kind of slapstick dispute.

"That's enough joking around."

"Who was joking?!"

"Our analysis of Dr. Glenn is correct. We don't lie. However, we also recognize that humor is a necessity when managing the graveyard city."

Molly happily fixed her clothing. Since her clothing was part of her body, she could have returned to her original state in an instant, without going through the motions of undressing or fixing her clothes. But this was part of Molly's mimicry process.

Even if she and Glenn didn't see eye to eye, Molly made every effort possible to learn about humans and monsters so she could assimilate. Glenn understood that, so long as she had that will, there would be no major problems. She was intelligent, she took others into consideration, and she knew it wasn't okay to cause harm. She was no longer the chunk of flesh that had lost its reasoning and attacked Lulala.

"If you are returning to the city, I have a request."

"Yes?"

"Because of our duties as manager, there is almost no opportunity to visit downtown Lindworm. Please tell the mermaid, Lulala, that I am living in the graveyard city." She went out of her way to name Lulala, proof that the mermaid was special to her.

"Why don't you go to town yourself? Lulala is always singing in the canal and the central plaza."

"That is not possible. We did the unthinkable. We threatened the Draconess Skadi's life and nearly ate Lulala. Even if the former was due to lack of knowledge and the latter was due to malnutrition, we should not be permitted in the city."

"But that..."

"Negative. This is not based on permission from others. We have drawn a line. Everyone in the graveyard city is the same. We are in the graveyard city because we can't go to the town. We made a decision, and we will stand by it." Molly seemed intent. "But the fact remains that we are all residents of the same town. Please tell Lulala that I am here."

"I understand. I'll make sure to tell her."

Molly put her hand to her chest—the chest she had just exposed. Perhaps she was feeling a heart that didn't have a flutter.

Or perhaps she put her hand on her chest because she was feeling the skeleton of the previous manager that she took into her shapeless body, thought Glenn.

"I am a fake."

"..."

"But I can read the previous Molly Vanitas's thoughts from her bones. It's not logical, but I have become Molly through her bones."

"Yes, I think I understand."

"I'll become an even better manager. I ask for your help in the future."

Glenn smiled. So long as she was around, the graveyard city would become a lively place. He waved back at Molly. Even if the she never came downtown, at least she would always be here.

This was the ending Dione and Skadi had hoped for. Glenn was sure of it.

"You look like you're enjoying yourself, Doctor."

"Well, I'm glad to be able to help Molly. I'll have more to do though."

"I'll make sure to keep a stock of preservatives. Ahh, we're so busy. We're so busy we don't even have time to go on a date."

"Uh..."

Sapphee was being passive-aggressive.

They could hear someone humming from the church; it was probably Molly. It sounded like a requiem. Maybe she'd learned it from Lulala. It was comforting, knowing they could come back and hear the doppelgänger singing at any time.

"Hey, Sapphee?"

"Yes?"

"How about we look at the lanterns just a bit longer before we go? We haven't been able to go out together much."

Sapphee looked surprised.

It was rare for Glenn to be the one to invite her out. And during the doppelgänger commotion, Glenn had worked a lot without her. He'd even been hospitalized for it, and, because of that, Sapphee had had to work harder.

"Just a little bit longer, Doctor. We have a lot of work to catch up on."

"I know."

Sapphee slipped her tail into Glenn's hand. The cool scales felt good against his skin.

The ghost lights that illuminated the dark graveyard were tranquil. Molly Vanitas's requiem resounded throughout the town, even as they walked away from the church.

× ✖ ✖ ✖ ×

Grave visits had become a hot topic among the residents of Lindworm.

People went to the graveyard city on the outskirts of town to mourn their dead. Rumor had it that if they asked the manager of the graveyard city, she would transform into the recently deceased so that the townsfolk could look upon the faces of those they'd lost.

The faceless doppelgänger, the mimic who could turn into anyone, the second-generation manager, Molly Vanitas, who lived with and protected the dead, was thriving, just outside the city.

Afterword

HELLO, I'M Yoshino Origuchi.

I don't know when you're reading this, but it's possible that we've already become a manga on the *Comic Ryu* website. The series will begin on February 26. Please read Kanemaki-sensei's bold and delicate comic depictions.

I went there. The graveyard city.

As a doctor, Glenn Litbeit can't avoid the problems of life and death. It might be fine if he were a normal doctor, but Glenn has undead patients too. He can't hold onto human notions of what it means to die.

What did you think of Glenn's approach to the undead perspective of life and death and his work in the graveyard city?

I would now like to express my gratitude.

To my editor, Hibiu-san, who is always watching over me. He has a habit of saying, "It's the end of the world," but it's all thanks to him that the *Monster Girl* light novels have made it to a fourth volume. Thank you.

Also, to Z-ton-sensei, who has illustrated the entire series! The goggle-eyed, expressionless, playing-dumb manager is just too adorable! Is it acceptable to have an unedited, exposed breast scene in a light novel? It is! It's just a medical exam!

Also, to Thomas Kanemaki, for handling the manga transition! I want to thank you for turning this work into a manga, even though it didn't seem suitable at first. I'm sure I'll be causing you many more headaches in the future.

Also, thank you to all the authors involved, the *Comic Ryu* reps, my family who gives me writing topics without even knowing it, proofreaders who find every teeny tiny mistake, and all of you readers. I am forever grateful.

Next, I think we'll hear more from some demons and Arahnia. Also, though we keep mentioning her, Aluloona has yet to make a meaningful appearance. We'll have to change that!

—Yoshino Origuchi

About the Author, Yoshino Origuchi

I like my monster girls with a lot of arms and without a defined shape. I also like the undead. I'd like to go on a date with an undead girl, someone who won't die easily.

If it sounds like I would date anything at this point, I'd have to agree.

About the Illustrator, Z-ton

We're becoming a manga!

It's probably going to be tough to design and draw characters when we've given no consideration to mass productivity...

I'm sorry, Thomas-sensei! I never thought it would turn out like this...